GONE FOR A

SOLDIER

Best Wishes

Norman Vigars.

Dedicated to my wife, Janet

About the author

Having written many documentary film scripts and articles on a range of subjects, Norman Vigars has published his first novel. A soldier in three campaigns in the last war, he found between brief moments of danger and long spells of boredom there was much humour and hilarity among his comrades.

An interest in eighteenth/nineteenth century history years ago led him to discover that nothing has changed.

In the latter part of the war he was an Army Photographer and was Mentioned in Despatches.

A seven-year spell as a photo/journalist in Fleet Street led him into the world of documentary films where he spent over thirty years until retirement.

He has lectured all over his native Essex, mainly to the over-sixties, on the subject of "Photo-Journalism In The Fifties".

He is married to a retired head teacher and has a son working in television. His love of music is kept alive by his daughter-in-law, a singer in the international operatic world.

GONE FOR A SOLDIER

by Norman Vigars

Peninsular Press

Copyright © Norman Vigars 1998
First published in 1998 by Peninsular Press
3a Blackacre Road
Theydon Bois, Epping
Essex CM16 7LT

Distributed by Gazelle Book Services Limited
Falcon House
Queen Square
Lancaster England LA1 1RN

The right of Norman Vigars to be identified as the
author of the work has been asserted herein in
accordance with the Copyright, Designs and Patents Act
1988.

ISBN 0-9534283-0-3

This publication is managed by Amolibros, Watchet,
Somerset
Printed and bound by Professional Book Supplies,
Oxford, England

Preface

The French Revolution began in 1789 and the revolutionary wars in Europe occupied the end of the eighteenth and on into the early part of the nineteenth century, until the Emperor Napoleon's total defeat at Waterloo in 1815.

The whole of Europe was involved as great armies moved back and forth and great sea battles took place on the Nile, at Copenhagen and off Cape Trafalgar.

Britain became involved through France declaring war in 1793. There was a brief peace after the treaty of Amiens in 1802 but hostilities began again in 1803.

The major involvement of a British army was in the Portuguese/Spanish Peninsular which started in 1808. First under Sir John Moore, and later under Wellington, the Peninsular campaigns became the centre of Britain's part in the European war. The turning point of 1812 saw Napoleon's defeat in his disastrous Russian adventure and the emergence of Wellington's army as a mobile and efficient war machine. These two events marked the end of Napoleon's ambition to rule the world.

Wellington's Peninsular campaign ended with the crossing of the Pyrenees into France in 1814 and the second brief peace until Napoleon's return from Elba in the summer of 1815 and the final chapter of Waterloo.

For Britain, the Peninsular War marked a distinct bridge between the eighteenth and nineteenth centuries. Large armies were raised and many young men went off in a spirit of high adventure - young officers, keen for a fight, for promotion and a welcome change from the social round of barrack life. In the ranks were weavers and miners from the North, ploughboys and shepherds from the Downs and always large numbers of young lads from impoverished Ireland, eager to go anywhere for fun, free drinks and the chance of being in on the sacking of a Spanish city.

At home the Industrial Revolution had begun and, in spite of financing her own armies, Britain was providing stores and money for half the allied armies including those of Prussia, Russia, Spain and Portugal. Britain was blockaded by the Napoleonic decrees and searched for trade outlets everywhere. Yet she managed to prosper and develop to a greater degree than any of the continental states.

Against this huge canvas the ordinary British soldier lived, marched and fought. He proved himself a better soldier than most of the allies although he had a healthy respect for the French. He was wiry, adaptable, resilient and very loyal. But he was also ready for fun and frolic whenever the opportunity came. Described in a moment of petulance by his Commander as "...the scum of the earth enlisted for drink", he nonetheless endured terrible privations of cold, heat, hunger, long marches and fierce encounters. Flogged for minor crimes and hanged for more serious ones, he still kept a sense of proportion about many things. Seldom paid, he looted with the best as natural recompense for his day's work. If he drank to excess it was as a reaction to harsh usage and conditions.

The Irish and their fantastic camp followers were the wildest of the lot.

This is their story: the ordinary soldier, his womenfolk and their adventures in the Peninsular almost 200 years ago.

Throughout the first half of the nineteenth century a number of books, diaries and letters were published giving firsthand accounts of the Peninsular War. These were written by officers and other ranks alike. All the "incidents" incorporated in this novel are drawn from research into such books.

CHAPTER ONE

The Recruiting March

The drum had an insistent note. It was sharp and its sound carried a long way. It was played simply; no tricks or fancy rolls, just a steady beat of one—one—one, two—three. The drummer sounded as though he were tired, or drunk. Both were possible.

The drum made the first announcement of its owner's purpose, but its companion, a high-pitched and distinctly off-tune fife was close behind. The tune was soon recognisable and although over a hundred years old was still popular in the England of 1811. Men had marched to *Sweet Polly Oliver* since the great days of Marlborough. It was heard at Culloden and the '45 with the redcoats' colours. In recent living – or near dying – memory, it had urged some weary feet a few steps further in the terrible retreat across Spain and Portugal to Corunna.

Heard now, at the approach to a quiet Dorsetshire village, it could only mean one thing; a recruiting party was on the march.

The silhouettes of moving figures in the afternoon sun were clearly outlined along a ridge. Upper parts were sharp, like a pen and ink drawing, but the lower

1

half of the picture was a cloudy swirl of dust kicked up by erratic feet.

At the head was the tall figure of the recruiting sergeant, made even taller by his black felt shako. Red coat and gold thread, wide, pipe-clayed crossbelts, brass buttons and tight breeches topping dark brown gaiters; these men were always magnificent sights and half their persuasion of the gullible young men was done for them before they opened their mouths. Recruiting sergeants were chosen from among the very fit and the well-built. They moved about with quick, lithe steps as they sold the army to a country boy. The colour and the sheer breath of fitness and good living were vital parts of their image-building campaign. They were among the first of the gentle persuaders.

Supporting this fine figure was a stunted but neatly turned out drummer boy. Small of limb and feature, he still looked a goodly complement to the sergeant, for he wore the gold frogged coat of a Regimental Drummer.

The fifer was a normal infantryman, wearing a modified version of the sergeant's outfit. He was not a regular army musician, but professing an unfounded skill with a flute, had connived to become the sergeant's right hand man. He had paid the sergeant handsomely for the privilege of joining the recruiting party on the promise of a share in the various cash benefits, regular free liquor and a month's absence from the rigours of barrack life.

These three were separated from their charges by a small pack-horse that carried kit, water canteens and some blankets. It was not done to reveal at too early a stage that soldiers carried most of life's necessities upon their backs.

Now the recruits themselves: a mixed bag totalling eight souls in search of adventure or escaping from a harsher life. They were still a long way from the regular marching rhythm of their leaders and most just shuffled along in an uneven and, in some cases, drink-fuddled fashion. Their midday meal had dragged on into the afternoon and the sergeant had been in generous mood at the last ale house.

First came three lads from the last village; shepherd boys in their late teens, they clutched small bundles of spare clothes, still wondering if this first momentous decision in their uneventful lives was the right one. Then came a tall raw-boned Scot, far south from his native hills and of solemn and quiet features. As he walked, he read from a small book and always managed to keep a few paces between those in front and those behind him.

Next came another tall, bone-sharp man, a Leicestershire weaver. He was unemployed and had been on the road for weeks throughout a hard winter. His clothes were thin and very worn, but he looked content, as though, at last, all future problems were going to be solved for him. He had already given up making any further decisions about life and the black half-bottle of rum provided by the sergeant was frequently helping him into a mellow state of oblivion.

Trotting beside the weaver was a small dark man in a black fustian suit that was several sizes too large for him. He had left gaol early that morning at the last sizeable town on the route. Having nowhere to go and not a penny on him, his immediate problems had been solved by a few brisk words from the sergeant. A quick check up with local gaols had provided many a man for the Peninsular War. The little ex-felon made frequent attempts to get his hands on the weaver's black bottle.

The rearguards were a strangely assorted pair. Irish Tom Eagan had led a vague and muddled life for nearly thirty years, mainly around his home in Clonmel. At an early age he had acquired a full-bodied taste for drink of any sort. In service as a boy and into his youth at a large Anglo-Irish country house, he had joined his fellow servants in the steady plunder of the master's cellars. Tom always took up a bottle, be it wine or spirits, raw or quality, as the most natural action in the world.

His contact with the gentry, even from the lower echelons of the servants' hall, had given him a taste for rich food and good living whenever the opportunity presented itself.

When fortune was good, he was as wild and roistering a blade as ever turned out of Ireland. When cold, hungry and shoeless or about to be thrown into gaol for one of his many convicted crimes, he had a philosophical way with him that usually ended in a song, a joke and a vow that before long he would be back with the good life again.

He was slim, lithe of build with a small mischievous face. He always managed to maintain a certain raffish appearance, even when his clothes were, as now, one short stage from a bonfire. In appearance he was in direct contrast to his companion, yet at heart there could not have been two more kindred souls.

Molly Eagan was as round as her husband was lean and wiry. She had been the pride of Clonmel in her youth and even now, approaching thirty, there were still traces of an early beauty. Some might have called her plump face comely, but the eyes under the tousled mass of dark hair had a wild, spirited fire in them.

A lifetime of living hand to mouth usually left women of her age looking ready for the grave - skin and bone, like so many Irish peasant wives. But a quirk of nature had left Molly with arms and legs, breasts and hips of more than generous proportions.

She had followed her wayward and graceless man through innumerable scrapes and adventures. They had even been to gaol together. When he took off to England in order to avoid a certain situation that had developed with the authorities in Dublin, she followed as a natural course. When Tom, half-fuddled with a stolen bottle of brandy, fell in with the recruiting team she too followed in the wake.

It was usual for the army only to allow wives to follow their husbands if the man was a regular soldier with some length of service. But Wellington needed men badly and all manner of blind eyes were turned when a new recruit insisted on his woman joining him. From a proportion of ten or a dozen wives per Company of a hundred men, the ratio was increasing with every draft.

Molly had heard of a number of her Irish sisters who were already in the Peninsular and the tales of loot, plunder and fine clothes usually outweighed the more truthful side of the stories and the attendant privations.

With a bottle in one hand and a half-gnawed ham hock in the other, she was skilfully perched on a minute donkey, a carpetbag of spare clothes and a few old sacks doing office for a saddle.

So the ill-assorted group topped the rise and turned down into the single street of Winterbourne, Dorset, in the early spring of 1811. The sun was in its third quarter of the day and now settling behind the bare trees that ran beside the road down the hill and into the village.

It was still very cold for late February, but the ground was dry and beginning to get dusty. The village street, like any in Dorset, or for that matter any in England, was little more than a dust track in summer and a lake of mud in winter. Here and there flat stones had been laid in rows in front of a few of the larger houses, the two shops and the inn.

Most of the cottages were stone and plaster or lathe and plaster with heavy thatched roofs. The inn, named as so many were at the time, The George, was a solid two-storied building with a wide courtyard at the side for stabling. It had been more lavishly built than its neighbours by the local squire in a fit of generosity at the time of the coronation and his own acquisition of a knighthood.

Life could have been worse in this early part of the nineteenth century: the predominantly agricultural way of the southern counties of England was rhythmical, satisfying and uncomplicated. Rumblings were heard about a new and industrial way of life that was changing the shape of the North of England. Men spoke of high wages in mines, factories and mills. But they also spoke of crowded towns, stinking slums and appalling long hours at the new machines, away from the sunlight and fresh air.

Winterbourne was a village closely tied to the local sheep farming and most of the cottages housed shepherds. These men and their sons were out from sunrise until after sunset on the surrounding downs with the fat, stub-tailed breed of sheep that had kept the district in a fair state of prosperity for nearly a century.

In the village the cottage doors opened at the sound of the military music, but some were shut tight again by those who quickly realised the purpose of the fife and drum. A few anxious mothers sent younger children running off into the fields to warn their older brothers to stay there until nightfall.

The rest of the village children, their quick ears catching the music approaching their houses, abandoned a game of squirting water over each other at the village pump and ran hallo'ing down the street.

At the door of her cottage, Mrs Wheeler looked out with mild interest and thanked God that four of her brood, clattering by with their friends, were too young for this soldiering business. Her eldest son, Jack was a different case. She turned to a neighbour who was looking anxiously up and down the street. "Have ye sent a kid up to long meadow to warn your Billy?" she asked.

The woman turned, wiping her hands on her apron. "I 'ave that, Mrs Wheeler. Soon as I 'eard they drums I knew 'twas Militia on the beat agin for poor young hands to the slaughter."

"'Tis so," said Mrs Wheeler. "Let's see, your Billy would be twenty-one year now, wouldn't he?"

"He's nigh twenty-two," said the woman. "I and my man 'ave no wish for him to go for a soldier. But what of your Jack? He's older'n Billy and more of a lively sort by far. Has he never wanted to go a'roaming agin or talked of joining the militia?"

"Several times," snorted Mrs Wheeler. "And we'd not stop him. I know his work brings in a few shillin' when he's around to do it. But it's the wenches keeps him here. Don't know where he get it from—his father's a quiet enough man, 'cept for the odd drop of spirit once a week at The George."

"Well, if he's not home I reckon the army'll 'ave to do without him," said the woman.

"Yes," murmured Mrs Wheeler, "and a few more broken hearts in Winterbourne before we get Master Jack to the altar with a decent wife."

They stood in silence at their respective doorways, one anxious and one meditative. The object of Mrs Wheeler's thoughts, her eldest son by eight years from her next child, was Jack. Twenty-three years old and born of a Dorset shepherd's family, he had helped his father in the sheep folds since the age of nine, after a brief three years at a village Dame school had completed his formal education.

At this stage he could count a little and read simple words. Encouraged by his mother, he later widened his knowledge by extensive reading. Starting with the church hymn books and going on to more advanced works borrowed from the village parson, he had become something of a prodigy among the largely illiterate folk of the district. He had also shown some dexterity with his hands from an early age and had picked up the craft of the cobbler between time spent tending sheep.

He had an insatiable curiosity for news and events from the outside world. Any passing tinker or peddler was always waylaid for gossip. To his uncritical mind all news was received, absorbed and digested, to be discussed later with the local lads at The George.

His country's war with Napoleon had fired his imagination, although it had been going on for most of his life and was accepted by the villagers as a normal and at times rather distant background to their everyday lives. As the most avid questioner and attentive listener in the village, Jack was recounted tales of brutish treatment and harsh conditions that changed even his romantic fancy for a life at sea.

The army seemed a different proposition. He had seen the militia on parade during periodic visits to Dorchester and had marvelled at the bright red coats, brass buttons and pipe-clayed accoutrements. He had stared with other visiting country boys at the gold-faced uniforms of bandsmen and drummers and had jumped about like a child to the music. The beautifully turned out officers on well-groomed horses had seemed Godlike beings from another world. The army had always been at the back of his mind as promising a fine and adventurous career for a young man of spirit.

Knowing little of the life that Britain's soldiers really led in that distant campaign of Spain and Portugal, Jack banged away at tattered village shoes and dreamed of a romantic idyll in the company of jolly roistering comrades. The image was a vague myth-filled atmosphere of tents, bugles, clean uniforms and occasional skirmishes with a shapeless mass called the enemy. These brief and noisy encounters of the imagination always ended in victory, the gathering of a few lightly wounded comrades and then pipe and glass round a roaring fire – not unlike an annual harvest bean feast up at the squire's big barn.

His curiosity, love of gossip and his agile brain set him apart from the local lads. But there was another side of him that made him, in turn, a subject of village gossip - his remarkable way with women.

Always a member of village activities, it was at just such a feast in the squire's big barn that started Jack, at seventeen years, on the road to the title of "Winterbourne Wencher".

Fuddled with cider, he had been dragged out to a hay rick by the even more drunken wife of the village blacksmith, an insatiable, well-built Amazon in her thirties. Their fumbling and confused encounter had not been unrewarding and the young man set about a series of conquests that soon exhausted the supply of willing young women in the village.

By the age of nineteen he had two local maids with child. One was sent in disgrace to London, the angry parents having grave suspicions about Jack, but the lovelorn girl refused to reveal her partner of a hot June night in the hedgerows.

The other had a stillborn child. It was after this scandal broke that Jack had caught the night mail to Dorchester and signed up apprentice to a cobbler in that town.

The cobbler had two young daughters and not many days passed before this busy and respectable household was a turmoil of feminine intrigue as the new apprentice did his best to please the women in the house. His master was suspicious from the start but, being lazy by nature, did nothing about it until, returning earlier than usual one evening from the local market, he found his bound apprentice far exceeding the articles of his indenture. In fact he was in bed with the mistress of the house.

Within three minutes Jack was picking up his few scattered belongings in the street and holding a rag to stop the bleeding from a wound at the side of his head. The cobbler followed Jack's baggage with a well-aimed iron shoe last, and the usual admonition never to darken his door again.

A few seasons helping local farmers at lambing time plus a bit of mixed cobbling and tinkering, such vagrant jobs kept Jack on the move for two years. He had carefully avoided coastal towns and the risk of the naval press gangs. He remembered when, a lad of seventeen, his parents had hidden him when a press gang swept through the village - pausing to grab two tipsy but inoffensive yokels. One never returned, but left a wife and four children as a burden on the parish. The other came back after four years, minus an arm and full of a black, bitter and cursing hatred for the sea in general and His Majesty's Navy in particular.

A very cold winter on the road had driven Jack back to his own village where his puzzled parents took him in again. The front room reverted to his cobbler's workshop and he settled down to the routine of village life. The scandals of his previous regime were soon being whispered around as this young romantic returned to his old ways.

With the sounds of drum and fife now much nearer, Mrs Wheeler's thoughts returned to her eldest son but the subject himself was half a mile away in a hay barn on the squire's farm. The sound of the military music had travelled over the cold fields and reached Jack as he buttoned his top coat.

His companion, Miss Betsy Calton, was still sprawled on a hay pile in a flurry of petticoats, looking very pleased with herself. Jack too had the flushed appearance of a young Casanova, for this conquest of only three weeks was his first excursion into the realms of high society. Miss Betsy was a niece of the squire's, sent to the country from her London home where it was said her wild ways in town were getting out of hand.

"What's that noise in the village, dear?" murmured the girl.

"That's a military sound, love. Might be a regiment on the move, tho' I've never known them come this way before. Anyways, I've seen the regiments marching in Dorchester and suchlike and they have a full band in tow. Sounds more like a recruiting party."

She sat up and straightened her clothes. "Recruiting party? Now that's not for you, is it Jack? You wouldn't desert a maid for a red coat and a musket would you?"

Jack grinned and teased her. "I might at that. Many's the time when I was a lad I've watched the soldiers in Dorchester and a fine life I've thought it to be."

She sat up in the hay and leaned forward to tug his coat. "All you'll get is a French musket ball in your guts, Jack Wheeler. I want you as you are, young lover; all in one piece and in good working order."

He straightened up at this piece of flattery, half thinking of himself in the bright uniform. He wasn't a bad figure of a man, he thought. Not tall, he was barely five feet eight inches, but with broad and powerful shoulders, chest and narrow in the waist. His features were evenly balanced and an unruly crop of dark hair gave him a Celtic look. There was a streak of vanity in him that went with his way with women.

She pulled his coat impatiently. "Why have you put on your coat, Jack? Stay a while longer with me for I've an hour before my sewing lesson up at the house. They'll not miss me yet, you know?"

"No, my little high-born lady. I must be away home, for I've done no work today. If it's true the squire is still in London for the rest of this week and your tutor woman or whatever you call her is spending her afternoons at the vicarage, then I'll meet you here tomorrow."

She pouted at him. "Tomorrow and tomorrow. How long can we go on like this, Jack?"

"Long as you like, Betsy my girl, but I've said it before, it can't go on for ever."

"Oh! My dear Jack," she cried, "what an age we live in. You men can take your fun and I'll not deny I like to join you in it, but a girl thinks of marriage. It's you I would marry if I had but half a chance. Why I'd even—"

He cut in sharply, "You'd what, Betsy? Elope with me over the hills to another town or village. Talk some daft parson into putting up the banns. Oh no! Not for Jack Wheeler and here's three points why. First, I'm not the marrying kind, not yet anyways. Second, you're squire's niece and I'm the son of Tom Wheeler, shepherd on your very squire's farm. It's not just in the nature of things for me to wed you. And there's the money side of things. I don't know how you're placed, but I've about five gold guineas in my savings and one good suit of clothes. So, I like you, Betsy. I like you more than any other wench in these parts. But I don't love you and I can't recall I've ever said I did. So there it is."

Betsy snivelled for a few moments, then brightened up. "I know," she said; "I'm eighteen in three months and come into my inheritance."

"And how much is that then?" said Jack.

"I don't rightly know, for tho' my father and my uncle have spoken of it, not exactly how much. But I'm sure it would be at least ten thousand guineas."

Jack sat down on a hay tip. "Ten thousand!" he gasped. "You'd get ten thousand! That could buy up the whole of Winterbourne village and enough to spare to throw a bean feast for all around."

He paused for a moment and did some mental arithmetic, partly to show off his superior schooling. "If my father saved every farthing he earned of his working life, he'd just about have ten thousand shillings, not guineas. My oath, Betsy, you're richer nor I ever thought."

She seemed pleased at this remark and said, "Well, Jack. I believe I could have one of my father's houses. Then I could set up and take you on as my footman or coachman or something. Then we could always—"

He cut in again. "I know what you're about to say. We'd always be together. Me touching my hat by day and creeping down the passages to your room at night. And how long d'you think that 'ud last? I'd give it about three weeks."

Betsy pouted again. "Well, I agree marrying you properly would be difficult. My father and uncle would be bound to make a great business of it and probably send me abroad at the first mention."

"Yes, and where'd they send me?" cried Jack. "I know, for I met a fellow once, in Taunton it was. Took in with a high-born lass. Got taken on as a groom at the hall. Discovered by the girl's mother when they were having a tumble in the stables, 'stead of out riding. Girl sent to London. My mate up before the magistrate, who, of course, was his master. Trumped

14

up charge, 'Guilty you rascal, transport him,' and that he was. To America, I think it was, loaded down with chains and there's an end to a lively lad if ever there was one. Oh, no! Not for Jack Wheeler, thank you ma'am."

"Well, Jack my lad," said Betsy, "perhaps you're right. We shouldn't dream of what we can't have. But I do find you such better company than those young fops my family are always bringing home to look me over."

Jack stood up and made for the barn door. "That's as maybe my jolly little Betsy, but you've my company for today. You must be to your sewing and I to stitching those damned old shoes." He peeped round the corner of the open door. "There's nobody about, so I'll slip away and you count to a hundred and be on your way. 'Til tomorrow, Betsy, same time."

He was out of the barn and running low, crouched low by a hedge before she could make any further protest. He straightened up at the end of the field and turned into a lane that led to the top end of the village. The drum and fife and shouting of the children were now much louder and curiosity set his steps towards the yard of The George Inn.

Already a small group was gathering there, knowing it would be the centre of events and, as Jack came to the yard gate of the inn, the recruiting party swung in with a final flourish on drum and fife.

The sergeant hammered on the side door and, as if in a play, the fat landlord came out with mugs of ale on a tray.

"Hallo, there, landlord!" cried the sergeant. "You've a quick head on your shoulders. Ale for these men. Look sharp now, bustle up. And a bottle of rum while you're at it."

The landlord distributed ale mugs around some oak tables, but as fast as he put them down, hands picked them up and the local brew went swilling down throats like rainwater in a storm.

"What about me, I've a thirst on me too, y'know. Get me down, Tom, by the Holy Lady, get me down. I'll miss me turn." The raw voice from atop the little donkey was bellowing for attention and Tom set about heaving his magnificent great wife into a standing position. The landlord was back with more ale and the rum bottle. The new recruits settled down on benches or hunkered down against the inn wall.

With a skill born of long practice, Eagan had got hold of the new rum bottle and managed a long swig before the sergeant jumped forward and grabbed it. "Steady now, me Irish beauty; you've a fair load on already."

The little Irishman swung round and in no time had the soldier's flute out of its case where it had been flung among the ale pots on the table. Jigging and fluting as only the Irish can, whether in or out of drink, he drew shouts of laughter from the knot of villagers that had drifted into the yard. From the gatepost, Jack looked on in wonder.

The sergeant was rummaging in a haversack and produced a rolled up poster, a hammer and some nails. "See here, all you fine young lads—gather round and read this—tell your friends—tell your neighbours—here's a chance for you to have a bit of fun and get a crack at old Bony!" He set about nailing up the poster on the yard gate and the villagers crowded round.

The poster had a style of its own, fine and florid. It might have been written by the sergeant, although his talents as a salesman were more evident in the field of oratory than literature. It said, in varying sizes of type…

Any young man who is desirous to make a

FIGURE IN LIFE and wishes to quit a

dull and laborious state in the country,

has now an OPPORTUNITY of

entering into a glorious time of EASE

AND INDEPENDENCE which he

cannot fail to enjoy in the service of His

MAJESTY KING GEORGE.

A hastily added footnote told of:

…Superior comforts and many advantages

The sergeant drew back to let such as could read near the poster. "What's the name of this place, lad?" he whispered to a boy in the front rank.

"Winterbourne, Sir."

"Good boy; pity you're too young." He then raised his voice and cried, "Now, look here, you young men of Winterbourne! King George 'as sent me specially down here to see you! Go to that Winterbourne, 'e said, and tell them strapping fellows I wants them in a smart red coat and to carry a musket along of the great Lord Wellington 'imself! Now come on, me lucky lads! Step up and take a drink with a sergeant of the Line and let's 'ave a good look at you!"

He threw some coins at the landlord. "Let's have some more ale, old cocky, or I'll have you doing the goose-step on Portsmouth barrack hard!"

While more ale was brought, Molly Eagan had been busying herself behind a bush where some washing had been hung. The garments were swiftly rolled up and concealed under the bulk of her many dirty petticoats. She strolled back into the yard, a picture of innocence and pointed at Jack leaning on the gatepost.

"There's a beauty for you, sergeant! 'Tis a fine looking man, for you!" She came up to him with swaying hips and tickled him under the chin. Jack winked slyly at her and almost instinctively put a hand on her shoulder. "Come on, sergeant!" she cried. "Get this one for me, for I fancies 'im!" and she broke into a gurgling giggle.

The sergeant brought a pot of ale over to Jack and, sizing him up as a more intelligent looking type than the more gaping yokels in the yard, spoke quietly to him. "What's your name, my man?"

"Jack Wheeler, Sir."

"You don't need to go calling me, Sir, we're all comrades in the army—'cept the officers. You 'ave to call them Sir. Me, you just call sergeant. Well, Jack, here's to you and how do you fancy a spot of fine good sport as a soldier?"

"I've thought about it," said Jack. "I've thought a lot about it. Many a time. The Militia, perhaps – at Dorchester. But somehow…"

The sergeant nodded in a knowing fashion. "I know. You've got a trade, no doubt. Can you read that notice?"

Jack nodded.

"I thought you might," he went on. "I said to myself, 'ere's a likely and clever chap, so I did."

The sergeant pulled out the rum bottle and tipped a generous portion into Jack's mug.

"Now drink up," he said quietly, "and here's to you, Mr Wheeler. Keep an eye on me and don't be moving from this yard. I'll look around these neighbours of yours and see who has a mind to joining us. But you're the stuff I really need. You've a head on you and a fine set of the shoulders. Damme! I'll have you a sergeant like myself before we've marched into Spain. Are you married, Wheeler?"

"No," said Jack with a grin. "I'm not married and I don't think I'm likely to be for some time yet." At the sergeant's question a roar of coarse laughter burst from the now growing group of villagers. "'im married! He's married to half the wenches under thirty in these parts, sergeant. 'e should be married to my Dorothy one time and a score of other lasses, the young rogue."

"Women trouble, eh!" said the sergeant, confidentially. "Well, I can solve those little problems for you, my lad. Come with me and you'll leave all those troubles behind you. Now if we go back to Spain—well, I've been there, see, and those Spanish beauties, oh my eye! They're so lovin' and so tender, so friendly an' willing to a bright young spark like yourself. Need I say more?"

He slapped Jack on the shoulder and gave him a knowing wink. Then he moved off to ply drink and sales talk to the now swollen group of local men who filled the courtyard.

A sprinkling of anxious wives and mothers had come on the scene worried that a mixture of drink at an unaccustomed time in the afternoon and the martial words of the sergeant would prompt their menfolk into rash and headstrong action. Jack took a mug of rum to a quiet corner of the yard and sat on an empty beer keg. His mind ran over the possibilities presented by this new situation. His latest amorous adventure was already entering that stage of tedium when he was ready to bid goodbye to his Betsy. Like those before her she was urging a more permanent liaison. He knew she realised that their difference in station made this impossible. As to the local girls, they would tumble in the hay on any warm night, but it was not long before they came pleading for a small golden ring to seal the bargain. He was bored with village life; tired of banging away at dusty and broken shoe leather. His wanderings so far had been mainly forced on him by circumstances and his own wilful way of taking his pleasure on the wing until the consequences caught up with him. He sipped the strong liquor and looked with bland interest at the mêlée around him. Then, his mind made up, he called to the sergeant—"I'm with you, sergeant! I'll take your shilling and anything else that's going."

"Well done, lad," said the sergeant. "Stick around for a bit, but we'll not be long in this place."

The young drummer and red coated fifer had taken up their instruments and were playing the march *Garryowen* for all they were worth.

Jack slipped away from the yard and hurried down the street to his parents' house. "This is it," he murmured to himself. "I've finished with the cobbling trade for a bit. Time to make a change. Let's have some fun and see a few sights while I'm still young."

The band played badly, but the villagers of Winterbourne were hardly judges of good music. The sergeant moved rapidly from man to man, filling tankards and collecting names. He paused once to order hot meat and potatoes from the landlord. "Enough for everybody," he shouted, "and ready in half an hour!"

He was a master at his craft and intended being on the road long before nightfall. Recruits, and particularly their kinfolk, had a way of changing their minds if you stayed around in the locality for too long. Time was running out on him and he was determined to work fast on this little situation.

Jack's mother had moved into the house as he had approached and, although he had not said a word, she asked no questions. She knew he had just made up his mind. In a way she was glad he was taking actions of his own free will and not fleeing into the night as before with a pile of trouble behind him. She trembled a little at the thought of him going to the wars, but folded her arms in a gesture of resignation.

Once in the living room of the house, Jack set about his preparations with a grim determination. He quickly gathered up his cobbling tools, some thread and a small wooden box of nails. He made the whole into a bundle, adding a pair of socks and a shirt. Picking up a large leather strap, he laid it out under his leather apron, rolled everything up together and strapped it tight.

He opened a drawer in his workbench and took out a small cloth bag of money. Taking out a single crown piece, he gave the bag to his mother.

"Here, Mother. My savings, for I'll not be wanting them now. I'm off for a soldier, a soldier of King George, so they tell me. If I make a fortune, I promise you half, but here's a little to help you while I'm gone."

A quick embrace with his mother, who showed a suspicion of tears for the first time in many a year, a wave to the younger brothers and sisters gathered round the door, and he was off, striding briskly down the street in the thinning light of the late afternoon.

Back at the inn yard when Jack strode in, the Eagans had by now got their hands on the food and fresh supplies of drink. There were shouts of laughter and snatches of song. Somebody had even thought of getting a wooden tub of meal for the pack-horse and Molly's long suffering donkey.

The sergeant was quickly tidying up the kit on the pack-horse saddle, even while it ate its feed. He looked up and greeted Jack as he came into the yard. "Are you with me, Wheeler? Are you for the road with us?"

Jack gave the sergeant a huge grin. In his own way he had thrown in his lot with the mixed crowd of recruits, and, like all men, was light of heart at the making of so big a decision.

"I'm on!" he said. "I'll go for a soldier and the devil take the rest!"

The sergeant gave him a huge slap on the back. "I knew you were the man! I knew it, soon as I set eyes on you! You're better nor most of this gang, but they'll have to do. Stick by me, Jack Wheeler, and I promise you a sight more fun and booty than you ever dreamed of in this tin pot of a village!"

The sergeant grabbed a pewter plate of hot beef and half-cooked potatoes in their jackets. "Get some food in you, and take what drink you want. If we don't hit a billet 'til late tonight, I've a reserve of good rum to keep us warm. Now I've got to get this little lot on the road in ten minutes, or half of them will be back to mother."

He bustled around the courtyard like a fretful hen. He had made one of the fastest hauls of his career in this village and was soon rounding up and encouraging a sheepish knot of six local lads, each with his small bundle under his arm.

As Jack sat on a bench eating the sergeant's hot food, he saw his father come into the yard, summoned from the fields by one of the younger children. "Hallo, Father, I'm glad you came for I'm off for a soldier and I would have grieved if I'd not said goodbye."

His father joined him on the bench and accepted the pewter mug that had been refilled with the inn's best rum. The older man took a good swig and turned to his eldest son. "Well, there's a thing my lad. You've been a devil in your time and no mistake but I wouldn't wish this on ye. Are ye sure 'tis what ye want?"

"Ay, father," said Jack. "I've thought it out and I feel the need for a change. A bit of fun and some travel to forin' parts like. Anyway, Squire and Parson are always telling us 'tis a patriotic thing to fight for old England, so I'm probably a hero now, 'stead of what they usually calls me."

"That's maybe so," said his father, "but they'll beat you Jack, so I'm told. They'll treat you rougher than the convicts in Dorchester clink. If you goes to this Spain or Portugal, you'll likely get a musket ball in your guts or even git yourself a corpse, I wouldn't wonder."

"Not me, Father," laughed Jack. "I'm much too fly for that. No, its a great feeling I have now. I'm free for a bit. I've seen Mother and given her all my money too, so you've a bit to spare in the house now. I've packed me traps and said my goodbyes. Leastwise, I've said it to those who matter."

His father stood up and drained the last of the mug of rum. "Ah! My oath! That was a good drop of spirit on a cold day. Well, Jack lad. No hard feelin' to ye, my boy. You was a good scholar and can write a fair hand, so take a pen to us once in a while and let us know ye're still alive. Bless ye, Jack, and the Gawd above keep ye safe."

They clasped hands firmly for a full five seconds, then the older man turned and half ran out of the yard, brushing his way through the crowd and back to his lonely work on the hillside.

Whilst paying the landlord at the side door to the inn, the sergeant heard above the general racket a muffled clucking from where the Eagans' donkey was tied to a post. Although now far gone in drink, an instinct, a movement of natural reflexes had made Tom Eagan grab a wandering chicken and stuff it live into a hessian sack.

"Lay off that, Tom Eagan!" roared the sergeant. "You'll have time enough for that when we get you to

Spain. You can loot 'til doomsday there, but right now you'll put that fowl back in the hedge and straighten up for marching orders!"

The grinning Tom let go of the chicken in the face of his wife who was standing on the other side of their donkey. She was furtively trying to cram into a sack a small stew-pot containing the remains of the cooked beef. Her reaction was the same for almost any given situation in her life – a wild shriek of laughter and a vigorous blow with the sack at her husband's head.

Drum and fife were now in position; the sergeant scattered a heap of small coins – mostly farthings – to the excited clutch of children in the yard, and the now considerably increased column set off down the village street.

It could not be called marching, for the steps were mixed to the extreme. The newest recruits were all together and fired by their new-found military pride were making some attempt at a regular rhythm. But the original recruits had had quite a day of it, one way and another, and were only concerned at keeping up with the main party.

Molly was perched unsteadily on the donkey, as before, but her now sleepy spouse was keeping going by clutching a handful of her dress, thus being half dragged along as a comic and ridiculous rearguard.

Most of the older menfolk of the village stayed behind at the inn to finish off the remains of the sergeant's generous donation of ale. The Winterbourne recruits were all, mercifully, unmarried; but a few anxious mothers trotted along the moving column with last minute pleas for a change of heart or with urgent advice about keeping dry and avoiding the loose women of the towns.

An early evening chill settled on the village. The only evidence that a recruiting party had been through was the diminishing sound of the drum.

The womenfolk gathered in worried little groups by their doorways.

The children huddled at the base of the pump, counting farthings.

CHAPTER TWO

Gone For A Soldier

Five days and twenty more recruits later saw the now stretched-out column of would-be adventurers clattering over the cobbles of the northern entrances to Portsmouth town.

Thirty-four, plus the dubious advantage of Molly Eagan's services, was not a bad haul for the recruiting sergeant. He had not done so well since the autumn of last year, when he had got in among a riotous wedding party at Brighthelmstone and picked up twenty-five revellers, joining them to an existing batch of a dozen others. He had managed to have the lot safety signed up in Horsham Barracks a day later.

Jack was at the head of the column, marching with the sergeant where he had enjoyed a number of confidences, a lot of advice and not a few privileges.

The drum and fife took up the merry step of the march, *Garryowen*.

"You'll not be long hanging about here, Wheeler," said the sergeant. "the 52nd have a near full draft down from Horsham Barracks and I'll tuck you little lot in with them."

"What about learning the trade?" asked Jack.

The sergeant grinned. "You'll have a few weeks in the Marine Barracks here while the draft gets kit and stores. They'll soon get you into shape."

Jack turned round and looked back down the straggling line to where Molly Eagan's tousled head bobbed along at the rear.

"Will Molly Eagan be allowed to take her donkey?" he asked.

"If I know Molly Eagan, she'll have sold that heap of skin and bone and Tom'll be in spirits for a week on the proceeds. 'Course she'll need some sort of baggage animal on the campaign. A mule probably. I'd like to see her on a mule. A lively one." He relished the vision for a moment as they swung into the side gates of the Marine Barracks and shambled to a halt by a large wooden hut.

The sergeant turned to his charges as the last note of the drum and fife shrilled away. He addressed them in the same paternal manner that had been his style throughout the march. It was in contrast to the harsh and guttural shouts that could be heard on the other side of the row of huts. From there came the stamp of many feet, the clatter of musket drill and a counterpoint of bugles and drill sergeants' voices.

"Now, me lads!" cried the sergeant. "You've done me well and marched like soldiers. A few details to be fixed and you'll be real soldiers and I reckon King George'll be proud of you. First—into line and one at a time through that hut door to see the doctor. Second—into that next hut four at a time and swear the oath before an officer. Third—into the next hut along the line and draw a blanket. Then I'll be waiting for you by the Sutlers' tents at the end of the line, where I'll buy you all a glass of grog for old time's sake!"

They formed into a rough and ready line with Jack Wheeler at the head.

"Hold your heads up straight, say 'Sir' to the doctor and speak up like gentlemen!" cried the sergeant. "In you go, boys and good luck!"

The sergeant strode off with his two assistants to record his list in the attestation hut and collect his bounty of two guineas per man. The days of marching on the recruiting drive had proved that he had no cripples on his hands. He knew the doctor well and was confident that anything less than a wooden leg would get by that enthusiast. Besides, the doctor was paid half a guinea for every man he passed and Wellington needed men.

The fifer kept close to the sergeant, for their original bargain had involved a share of the prize money and the balance of the expenses allowance.

Back at the medical hut, Jack was the first through the door.

It was barely furnished with a couple of tables and benches. On a high backed chair at one end Doctor Skillen sprawled with a glass of brandy in one hand and a short riding whip in the other. An orderly sat by the first table and a duty sergeant strode about the room, swishing a swagger cane with an air of some impatience.

"Come in, my man!" cried the sergeant. "Your name?"

"Wheeler, Sir."

"Don't call me Sir, I'm a sergeant. Call the doctor Sir!"

"Right you are, sergeant," said Jack, with a cheery grin.

"First name?" asked the orderly, writing laboriously on a piece of stiff paper.

"Jack. Jack Wheeler."

"Where're you from, Wheeler?" asked the orderly.

Jack told him, spelling out the name of his village with some care.

"Come on, come on!" called the impatient doctor. "I haven't got all day. Make them give their names while I'm examining them. If any are near death, I'll save you some trouble. Come over here, man!"

The sergeant led Jack across the hut, intoning the routine formula. "Jacket and shirt off, shoes off, lower your breeches when the doctor tells you."

The doctor turned in his chair as Jack hurriedly removed his upper garments.

"Take a deep breath—in, that's right. Now breathe out—good! Any colds, ague, coughs? No? Good! You look fit enough. Feet all right? Good! Have a look at his head, sergeant."

The sergeant prodded Jack's head in a vague fashion with his cane. "Looks all right, Sir," he said.

The sergeant stood back a pace. "Clean limbed man, Sir. No fleas or bug marks on him." He moved round to the side of Jack.

"Touch your toes, Wheeler!"

Jack bent smartly down, only to receive a stinging blow from the sergeant's cane. He leapt upright like a spring trap and turned quickly to the sergeant. "Damn y're eyes! You'll not catch me again like that."

"Shut y're mouth," barked the sergeant.

"Good," murmured the doctor. "Alert man that, sergeant; quick responses. He'll do. Orderly, give him his papers and get the next rascal in."

The sergeant took Jack by the arm, the latter trying to gather his scattered clothes around him. "You'll do, Wheeler. No offence, man. Just the sort we need.

Wait outside 'til I send three more out and you take them to the next hut where you'll swear for a soldier. After that you're really one of us. Off you go!"

The little gaol bird in his ill-fitting suit was next. At one stage there was a hurried whispering between the doctor and the sergeant.

"Come over here, man!" called the sergeant, indicating some white painted marks on the wall.

The little man was pushed against the wall and at the same time the sergeant deftly slid a flat wooden box into position with his foot. "Stand up straight, now," said the sergeant, indicating with his cane that the box was there for a purpose. The sergeant peered at the wall markings as the recruit stepped blithely on to the box. "Just right, Sir!"

"I thought my eyes didn't deceive me," said the doctor. "He'll do."

Outside, Jack had managed to get his clothes straight and was reading the piece of paper that had been thrust at him. He noticed the doctor's signature at the bottom, but could not remember the paper ever being passed across for this formality. They were obviously very efficient here.

After one of the Dorset villagers had been passed as fit, Tom Eagan skipped into the hut. The group outside listened with some glee to an altercation which included the doctor roaring something about "…get some soap and water on that man, sergeant. I can smell him from here!"

In a remarkably short space of time, the first four had been passed fit to bear arms and Jack led them into the attestation hut. The layout here was almost identical to the medical hut; a smartly turned out young officer occupying the same type of high-backed chair behind a table at the far end. A row of tattered bibles lay on the front of the table. To the right sat another orderly compiling the list of newcomers from the recruiting sergeant's scrawled notes. An even fiercer looking sergeant strode around the room.

"Step up smartly, lads and hats off to the officer!" he cried. "Let's have your names, calling from the right!" Jack called in a clear voice, followed by the others. The sergeant, wasting no time, collected their medical papers and gave them to the orderly who was busily compiling payrolls and recording the simple details of each man. Bureaucracy was at work, for in those days the army was years ahead of the central or the very rudimentary local government in the keeping of personal records.

The sergeant moved briskly to the table and handed out bibles. "All passed fit by the doctor, Sir!" he cried.

The handsome young officer looked up from a letter he was writing and eyed the recruits for the first time. "Good," he drawled. "They'll do. Now pay attention, you men. Repeat the words of the oath after the sergeant and stand up straight as you say them."

The sergeant chanted the phrases from long habit and the four men repeated them more or less correctly. "I swear by Almighty God – that I will faithfully serve His Majesty, King George the Third – his heirs and successors…fight to defend his causes…on land or at sea…defeat his enemies…be obedient to his officers and do my duty at all times."

Tom Eagan managed to muddle his words around, and muttered some lines of his own at the reference to King George. Nobody paid any attention, even when he concluded with a murmured "...and God save Ireland!"

"That's it!" cried the sergeant. "Bring their papers up, orderly. Write your names or put your mark at the bottom, men."

As the pen was passed from hand to hand, the officer handed out a shilling to each man and a slip of paper entitling them to draw recruits' bounty from the paymaster – the princely sum of ten guineas.

This apparent generosity was of a dubious nature for the paymaster was a man rarely seen by the rank and file. On the few occasions that the money chests came down from London the sums available were barely sufficient to pay the Commissariat for food, equipment and barrack bills. Small sums were doled out to the sergeants for Company expenses. Although a number of bolder recruits attempted to cash their bounty chits, they were invariably told – "bounty payouts next week."

Many a body in a shallow grave in the Peninsular became a simple entry years later – "Died on active service—all accounts cleared." It was rumoured that the paymasters made agreeable sums of money from unpaid bounties and were able to retire to their country houses in a coach and four.

The sergeant straightened up and addressed the new defenders of Britain's cause against the continental enemy. "You men have done a good day's work today. You've become soldiers of a fine regiment—the 52nd Infantry. Your regiment is soon to go off to join the great Lord Wellington, so work hard at your training and you'll be picked to go along with the draft. Any scrimshanking, thieving or neglect of duty will be punished—punished hard. Do your duty, and you'll not go far wrong. Right, sergeant—bring in the next!"

"Sir!" bellowed the sergeant. "Outside, you men. We've a lot to swear today!"

They hustled out, grinning and joking to the group of others waiting their turn to sign away their lives into the unknown. The system was working smoothly.

Jack and his three comrades made their way to the stores hut where each collected a new blanket. Tom Eagan immediately wrapped his around him like a cloak. "'Tis a cold day yet, Jack." he said. "Now wasn't that a nice little ceremony? I like things proper and ceremonial, like. Now where's that sergeant who was promising us a drink, for I'm fair ready for one after all those speeches and doctors prodding around me?"

They strolled past the huts to a cluster of large canvas tents. Damp wood smoke billowed from some open fires upon which large stew-pots were set.

The area was a bustle of soldiers, their wives, odd camp followers, moneylenders and the universal providers of those days – the sutlers. Frequently in teams of husband and wife, they moved in whenever troops were assembled in numbers; selling them drink, food, spare clothing and worthless trinkets.

The commissariat of the army was, by and large, efficient and supplied most necessities for a soldier's life. But since the days of the Roman legions on the march across Europe, there had been these bands of adventurers ready to trade, sell comforts and tag along with a soldier wherever he went. Many made their fortunes, even from the poorly paid soldier.

A shout from the recruiting sergeant, perched on an upturned barrel, brought the four over to where tin mugs were ready for the promised nip of rum as a parting gift.

"Well, boys," said the sergeant, "so you've made it. Soldiers of the King, eh! Now who's ready for a drink? First come, first served! When the whole of my little lot is here, I'll take you to your hut and hand you over to my old friend, Sergeant Hooper. He's a good man and will kick you into shape in no time. Give him no lip and he'll teach you your trade quicker than any man I know!"

He rattled away as he poured them each a drink. Tom Eagan, first in line with his tin mug, asked the sergeant if he'd seen Molly.

"She's off down the town to a horse meat dealer, selling that wreck of a donkey you brought along."

"Then I hope she comes straight back to barracks," said Tom. "She's a way with her if she's any money aboard and I need some cash for I'll not get far on this shilling."

The party grew and was finally marched off past a row of huts flanking the permanent brick buildings of the barracks. They moved by the side of a large gravel beaten square where groups of redcoated soldiers were being drilled. Here were those time-honoured patterns an army uses to move bodies of men as a disciplined, coherent whole.

A few more shuffled steps and the mixed clad draft were soon passing through the storerooms in the main barracks. A whirlwind of bewildering objects was hurled at them with the army's usual disregard for variations of size. In a matter of minutes, Jack and his comrades staggered across to the clearing by their hut, burdened like pack mules but excited by their newly won treasures.

"Here's a thing!" cried Tom, "I niver had so many things give to me at one go, and all free, gratis and for nothing. 'Tis a handsome thing we've done this day!"

They laid out their treasures in little heaps, turning things over, putting on jackets and trying to fathom the tangle of rough leather straps and the many dull brass buckles.

Jack, deciding that he had better tackle this chaotic mass of possessions by some method, laid out his blanket and distributed everything on it. A knapsack with belts and cross-straps, a wooden water canteen, tin mug, plate and spoon, two pairs of socks, two pairs of shoes, some coarse underclothes and an even coarser grey cotton towel: a razor, piece of soap, two candles, a packet of needles and thread, two shirts, a pair of blue/grey trousers – this a new issue for the tight breeches and gaiters were fast dying out. The jacket was the bright star in this rather drab mixture; scarlet, with some gold thread worked in at the shoulders and tails, it was of stout cloth with a fine array of brass buttons – all stamped with the regimental number – 52.

Jack tried his on and was surprised to find it more or less fitted. Tom Eagan's was several sizes too large and he capered about, shrieking with laughter like a clown in a circus. The tall, raw-boned Scot looked like a scarecrow with coattails not even covering his behind and wrists protruding from the short sleeves. A quick change with Eagan redressed the balance and similar swaps were going on all round the hut.

A corporal strode up to the busy scene leading three heavily laden soldiers carrying over a score of muskets between them. "Here you are, my lucky lads!"

he shouted. "Come and get your muskets, come a' grab hold of old Brown Bess! Any skylarking about 'til you've had some drill and I'll take the hide off your back!"

The long flintlock musket that had served the army for many years was an immediate source of interest to the recruits. The weapons were passed from hand to hand until each man had his own. A private doubled up to distribute the foot long, thin bayonets that completed the basic arms of infantry of the line. Later they would draw their brass box of leather patches, the twisted paper cartridges and that burden of all who marched to the drum and fife – sixty rounds of ball ammunition. It was considered prudent to withhold the lethal parts of the weapon until at least some rudimentary training had been carried out. Recruits with a little drink on board and flushed with an early pride in their regiment were liable to do serious damage to themselves or their comrades at their first handling of gunpowder.

As it was, two lively young sparks discovered how the bayonet fitted on the muzzle of the musket and were soon engaged in a warlike demonstration of close combat with parry and thrust. Tom Eagan's shouts of encouragement brought the corporal back and the two enthusiasts had their heads knocked together as a warning against further displays of military zeal.

The recruiting sergeant came up at this point and ordered his flock to gather up their belongings and follow him. Loaded like pack mules and leaving a trail of odds and ends behind them, they stumbled after him to the barrack hut that was to be their base from now on.

At the door of the hut stood Sergeant Hooper of the 52nd, a tall, lined, sunburned man with the unmistakable air of a veteran. He had served in Flanders and the ill-fated Walcheren expedition. His first stripes had been pinned to his sleeve after the successful battle of Maida in Italy in 1806. He had marched under Sir John Moore in the Peninsular and had survived the terrible winter retreat to Coruna in 1809.

Now he looked at the approaching shambles of the new recruits and prepared himself for a few short weeks of intensive work to bring them up to at least a reasonable state of worthiness to take the field.

The recruiting sergeant brought them to a halt and Tom Eagan collapsed in a heap of clothing and equipment. Hooper waited a few seconds for the Irishman to get on his feet and then addressed them in a quiet yet penetrating voice.

"Welcome to my Company. I'm Sergeant Hooper – your sergeant from now on. Your mother and your father, and nursemaid too I shouldn't wonder. I'm an old soldier and I know my trade. I'll teach you some of it and I'll teach you fast—fast and hard. Do as you're told and do your duty and no harm'll come to you. Play me up or play up the army and you'll wish you'd signed on with the devil. Now into your billet and sort yourselves out. I'll be along soon with a corporal to show you how to dress as a soldier and to clean your kit. You've plenty of coal and you draw your rations on the Depot bugle call. The rest of the day's your own, but don't go too often to those grog sellers' huts for tomorrow we start work at daybreak. In you go, you sons of Satan!"

They piled into the hut while Hooper and the recruiting sergeant marched off to those same grog sellers that were considered such a bad influence for new recruits.

The hut, furnished with Spartan simplicity, had two closely packed lines of narrow, wooden beds, some of them double tiered. At the end of the room was a large iron stove. A small table in the centre, a few pots and pans and a large iron bin of coal completed the entire contents.

Although new to the service, there was already an instinctive rush for the beds nearest the stove. Jack hurled his bundle on to a single bunk a quarter of the way down the room and next to a lad from his own village. Only Tom Eagan hung back until all had staked their claim. He then set up home on the bed nearest the door, shouting to Jack, "Oi've always a mind to being near the door. You niver know when youse want to get away in a hurry!"

Brief friendships had sprung up on the recruiting march, but here the small groups sorted themselves out into a more permanent pattern. Each group a mess in its own right, sticking together, quarrelling, getting drunk and swearing eternal friendship. They helped each other out in a rough and ready fashion and always referred to themselves as "...the boys in my mess." Between Tom's bed by the door and Jack's bed were four of their messmates: George Bates, a huge immensely strong ploughman from Dorset, over thirty years of age and a widower from the early part of the winter. With his three children in the care of his more prosperous sister - her husband kept a butcher's shop - he had taken the shilling with the rest of them. "...'twould be a bit of a change like and maybe I'll make me fortune." He was quite a loveable soul - a trifle simple and something of a butt for the quicker wits like Jack and Tom. Next was the little gaolbird who had joined the sergeant's column the morning of the march into Winterbourne. Christened in an orphanage, Richard Dewsbury he had been known since a vagrant childhood as Dick Dewdrop, a name that caused great amusement among his new comrades. He had been progressively chimney sweep's boy, crow-scarer, travelling tinker and a score of other callings. He was the only one among them who had been to London and frequently boasted of the raree shows he had seen around the stews of Drury Lane. He had a quick wit, a taste for strong liquor and boasted a wide range of bawdy songs learned when a ballad seller in London.

One bed up and sorting out straps and buckles with hands the size of York hams was Harry Wilkins, another huge ox of a man. He was every inch a townie. He had been apprenticed to the blacksmith's trade and while still a young man had moved from his native village to work at an iron foundry in Derby. He often held the simple country boys in awe with tales of giant furnaces and great troughs of molten iron. He also had a greater capacity than most for ale.

The last of this band whose bed was wedged between Wilkins and Jack was little Billy Kelp, seventeen years old and also from Winterbourne. He was already looking to Jack to help him with his kit. Soon nicknamed "Little Billy", this shy and nervous lad was only comforted by the fact that there were a number of others of his kind around him. In spite of this, however, it seemed strange that he had attached himself to the most rumbustious and fun-loving of the groups. Perhaps he felt a greater security with these tough but friendly messmates.

In the hut the rough straw mattresses were shaken out and kit distributed. Some wood was brought to start the stove and all was a bustle and chatter.

Jack had his kit straight in a few minutes and walked to Tom Eagan's untidy mess of a bed space. "Come Tom, let's have a walk round and I'll buy you a pot of ale."

Tom was up in a second at the talk of ale. "That's a great thought, Jack, but I'll not be wasting too much time for I need to hook up wid that great lump of a wife of mine. If she's sold that nag, I'll want to get me hands on the money before it all goes."

They strode off by the side of the great barrack square. The Marine Barracks was being used as a marshalling area for Peninsular reinforcements and apart from the regular depot of Marines, there were drafts for half a dozen different line regiments drilling under the sharp eyes and powerful voices of the drill sergeants. Jack stopped and stared in wonder at a full Company of the Rifles, the famous 95th, striding by in the double-quick time that was the marching pace of this crack regiment. Dark green jackets with black facings and black straps was their uniform, making a sharp contrast to the redcoated line regiments. Bugles gave them their drill signals – the only regiment to use them for this purpose.

Jack was fascinated and off again in one of his daydreams. He asked himself if he had done the right thing – joined the right set or would not there be more dash and adventure with these spirited looking men. He was to see a lot more of the Rifles in the next few years; watch them move out as skirmishers in front of the solid red squares, swooping and diving like snipe in a cornfield. Bugles rallied them, for the normal infantry drum would have been too cumbersome for such light troops. The new Baker rifle, smaller, faster and more accurate than Brown Bess, was a killing weapon in these sharpshooters' hands.

"Was you going to buy me this pot of ale, or are you after signing up wid this lot?" asked the impatient Tom.

Jack turned away, saying, "I'll stick with you, Paddy, we'll see a thing or two yet before we've done."

"We will that," laughed the Irishman, "but I've some business to get on wid when I catch that cow of a wife I've brought wid me!"

"What business would you do in this barracks, Tom? Nobody has any money here. Dicky Dewdrop and I tried to get our bounty from that paymaster fellow but his orderly says to come back next week."

Eagan screwed up his little face in disgust. "You'll have to stick by me if you're to survive, I'm thinking. Didn't I hear one of the lads say the sergeants collect all the old civil clothes from the recruities and sell them in the town. Well I've a thought to getting in first with a bit of business of that sort. This Sergeant Hooper seems a fine old boy – for a Sargint, but my Molly could be down in Portsmouth and sold our fellows' rags before the sun's on the clock tower tomorrow morning—and we'd share out wid all concerned."

Jack gave his mate a shove as he roared with laughter. "You're a rogue and no mistake!" he cried.

"You stick by me, boyo, me and Molly, and you'll niver want for vittles or a drop for your poor ould throat."

They walked off together in the direction of the sutlers' canteens, a strangely assorted pair.

The next few weeks were the busiest yet most exciting the recruits had ever experienced. Jack's quick intelligence stood him in good stead when it came to learning the complicated drill movements that were used to move a hundred largely illiterate men as a disciplined body. They stamped their feet, they wheeled and turned; at first in a ragged ill co-ordinated way but soon even the dimmest of them got the rhythm of keeping with the right hand marker. The drill sergeants and sergeant majors roared and bullied, chivvying their men like cattle drovers until out of chaos emerged order and neatness of movement.

They drew cartridges for their muskets and in open fields near the barracks learned the intricacies of "Look to your muskets…prime your muskets – ram your charge…etc….etc.," until the final words of command produced ragged volleys that crashed around ears unaccustomed to such sound.

There was grumbling from a handful of the recruits, but mostly there were few regrets so far for that hasty decision to take the shilling those few weeks ago. The food was coarse but plentiful. Beer money was a penny a day and some of the more enterprising who discovered illicit sources of additional income would often provide stronger drink for impromptu share-outs and parties.

Tom Eagan was frequently in funds and just as frequently out of them, for he was a generous man with his friends, if unscrupulous with the rest of the world.

Molly had sold her donkey and set up as laundress, cook, middleman and dealer for half the barracks. A natural leader, her strong character and unquenchable sense of humour soon put her at the head of the clutter of wives and camp followers who hung around the barracks.

The men did not want for female companionship during off-duty hours, for Portsmouth had one of the largest populations of professional and amateur prostitutes of any city in England.

Molly was mixed up in everything, even dealing in a little procuring of some of the newest women to the district for what she called, "...some of me favourite boys!" It was an act of generosity on her part that led to an ugly scene with her husband. She persuaded a fiery young Irish redhead to link up with Jack on the grounds that he looked lonely one evening and this was just the girl for him.

But Jack Wheeler was already satisfying his more basic needs with Sally Kinchin, unofficial wife in barracks to Corporal Kinchin whose duties as colonel's orderly kept him working twelve hours a day attending to his master.

Thinking Molly was with some of the other wives in the barrack kitchens, Tom Eagan took the redhead in tow to be discovered in a nearby hayloft by his enormous and very angry wife. His black eye and battered shoulders were a source of much crude laughter in the barrack hut as he declared, "...he'd rather taken two hundred lashes at the triangle than face the punishment ould Molly had dished out!"

Early one morning the drums of all the regimental drafts greeted the day with "Beat to General Inspection." "This is it!" the men said as they strapped on equipment, rolled blankets and fastened their greatcoats.

In Sergeant Hooper's hut all was confusion. Tom had lost or sold a good deal of his equipment and was bellowing for assistance. "Bates, me dear ould fellow, 'ave ye a bit of rope or somethin' to help hold this pack together?" George Bates got to work on the little Irishman with a heavy hand. "Stand still" he cried, "you're like a pig at market. I've a bit of cord here. Hold y're head up. So! Steady now! There I've lashed it round under your knapsack and blanket. They'll not be noticing your sprigged together like a Somerset mummer's horse."

Little Billy Kelp was being pulled and drawn together by Jack in an attempt to make the lad presentable and avoid him getting a dozen lashes at the triangle. "Come on, lad!" cried Jack. "You're nearly as bad as our Tom. What've ye been doing to these buckles? They're far too loose. You'll fall apart like an old mare on her last foaling. Give 'ere boy! Hold your breath now. Head up. That's better!"

With Sergeant Hooper now ready in the doorway, the band of soldiers clattered out to the barrack square.

An unknown but aristocratic looking general was mounted on a thoroughbred chestnut and surrounded by a group of foppish staff officers and the lieutenants who were accompanying the drafts.

The party rode down the lines of soldiers, stopping occasionally when a veteran was produced from the ranks. Very few Peninsular wounded ever got back on to active service, so the inspection was little more than a formality.

The General wheeled his horse in front of the main column and addressed the troops. Jack and his friends never heard a word from their position out on a flank, but were kept in good spirits by the mimicry and slanderous comments from Irish Tom. A surreptitious blow from the flat of a sergeant's sword cut short the comedy. In any case, Jack and his mate reasoned it was probably another of these exhortations to be good boys and do their duty. They were getting a little tired of talk and keen to get on the move.

The drums took up their beating again and a regimental band marched round to the head of the column, taking the long lines swinging out of the barrack gates in fine style.

Although the Portsmouth locals had seen this sight a hundred times, they still turned out to cheer, throw flowers and shout ribald comments to the passing redcoats.

Back in the barracks there had been a long argument between the wives of the troops and the orderly sergeant for the draft. Although the official number of six wives per Company was often stretched to ten or more, there was a particularly large number of women with husbands in this draft. So with the aid of the pay sergeant, a number of cards were put into a hat marked **TO GO** or **NOT TO GO**. The anxious women came up one by one and determined their whole future for themselves at the single drawing of a card.

Molly Eagan was one of the first to draw and triumphantly waved her ticket to join the troops. "They'll not get far without me!" she cried. "Who'll join me at the cook-pots?" The unlucky ones set up a great howl of protest and pleading. As it was, over a dozen slipped in with the authorised group and they all shuffled out with their baggage tied in blankets, looking like the tail end of a travelling circus.

Not a few of the others who had drawn **NOT TO GO** cards somehow managed to bribe longshoremen to ferry them out to the more distantly moored transports, enabling them to smuggle themselves aboard with the last minute loading of provisions.

Down on the hard at Spithead it was an impressive sight as the draft split up into Companies. They moved in colourful streams into the long boats that ferried them across to the transports and converted warships. Most of the soldiers, coming from towns and villages, had never seen such a forest of masts and such bustling and heaving before. The sailors had their own greetings for their land-based comrades and these were, for the most part, obscene or derisive.

The awkward, heavily laden troops were in direct contrast to the nimble, bare-footed sailors who heaved and pushed the soldiers up the sides of the ships like sacks of meal.

Jack and the boys of his draft were on one of the largest vessels – the *Revenge*. Sorting himself out on the deck he read out the names of the nearest ships to their own, impressing the mostly illiterate around him. There was *Samaritan, Matilda, Fortune, Laurel* and the *Malabar,* all now swarming with redcoats and gently rolling in a light swell.

Shouts and Bosuns' pipes, creaking and grinding of timber, the quick mysterious movements of sailors skilled in handling the apparent tangle of ropes and canvas; all this went on around the tightly packed troops who watched with growing interest.

Then a bull-like roar came from the quarter-deck of *Revenge* and a tall, gold-ringed senior naval officer made his presence felt. "Get those blasted redcoats below—damme, I'd sooner carry cattle. Get them out of here 'fore we up anchor or they'll have us on our side!" Bosuns and army officers bustled the men down companionways to the dark, damp holds that were to be their homes for the next ten days.

In a few hours the ships took on a rhythmical movement and the convoy was on its way in the gathering dusk with a full moon coming up over the horizon.

The voyage was uneventful, except for the usual squalls in the Bay of Biscay. Rough seas and sickness made the cramped quarters for the troops squalid in the extreme. But as soon as calm weather came, the soldiers were allowed on deck in groups for several hours each day. The troops were always glad to be up when the evening pipes sounded *Hands to Play* and they would watch the sailors dancing to pipe and fiddle, engage in friendly wrestling matches or squat down to yarn with the soldiers and share a pipe of ship's tobacco.

It was a good ship by the harsh standards of the time. One morning a rumbling drum note from the *Samaritan*, half a mile on the port beam, indicated a flogging in progress. The sailors on the *Revenge* told their army comrades how they thanked God for the stern but fair-minded captain of their ship who only resorted to the cat o' nine tails in cases of serious crime. Some captains considered their day's duty incomplete without at least one luckless sailor being beaten to insensibility.

Ten days and nights passed of a closely confined period in the soldiers' lives. They dreamed of home and talked endlessly of setting foot on dry land again. The soldier is always a bit of a stranger to the sea.

CHAPTER THREE

Peninsular Baptism

On a fine morning in the middle of April the line of transports shortened sail and dropped anchor in Figueras Bay, Lisbon. The Portuguese capital looked bright and inviting to the troops who were more than anxious to get on dry land again.

The high-prowed local fishing boats came out in swarms to take men and stores ashore and Jack, Tom and the rest of their mess were soon scrambling into the boats and grinning at the dark skinned Lisbonese fishermen.

A line of breakers crashed on to the beach and the crowded boatloads of soldiers viewed this with some misgiving. It looked like a wet landing ahead.

A long line of women was forming up on the edge of the surf - a sort of reception committee. Large and lusty fishermen's wives with their black hair tied in kerchiefs and their coloured petticoats tucked up to their waists. As the boats came within a dozen yards of the shore, the line of women waded sturdily through the surf and grasped the sides of the plunging boats.

"Come, Inglish soldier, climb on my back! One shilling and you no get wet!" The troops were at first amazed at the prospect of this piece of local enterprise, but a sergeant in the bow of the leading boat stood up and shouted, "Come on you men, don't insult a lady. Give her a shilling and you'll get ashore without a ducking!" So saying, he climbed with full kit on the broad back of the nearest fisherwoman. She heaved him up like a sack of coal and waddled ashore, collected her due and was back in a matter of seconds for another customer.

The whole scene was filled with boatmen's cries, the shouts of the women and rolling laughter from the troops at this unexpected piece of skylarking. Tom Eagan declared it the finest thing he'd ever seen. "Where's that fat cow of a wife of mine?" he cried. "Sure I could put her to work among this lot and make me fortune before nightfall!"

He was seized by an amazon who was of similar proportions to his wife and held aloft like a child as he was rushed through the surf.

Eagan seldom paid for anything on principle and was pleading abject poverty when his female bearer lifted him from the water's edge and was prepared to hurl him back into the sea. Eagan paid.

The men stood and cheered as the military wives were brought ashore from one of the last boats. But the women of Lisbon balked at carrying Molly Eagan through the waves. She was of proportions too similar to their own.

Molly stood up in the boat with a bundle of belongings as large as herself and shouted to her husband who was trying to hide behind a group of his comrades. "Tom Eagan, you devil, how d'ye think I'm to get ashore through this raging ocean? Have ye no thought for me, man?"

The soldiers had a quick consultation and persuaded two of the strongest fishermen to go out and get Molly. She perched on their shoulders like Britannia ruling the waves, shrieking with laughter and swaying with her enormous bundle. Halfway from the boat the co-ordination of the two fishermen broke down and all three plunged into the foaming surf.

Surfacing in about three feet of water, Molly's laughter had changed to a stream of abuse as she fished around for her scattered bits and pieces and waded ashore in a billow of soaked garments.

The troops formed up and were marched through the city, looking to right and left at their first encounter with a foreign land.

Jack and little Billy, Bates, Wilkins, Dewdrop and Tom walked along together, shouting with excitement at the scene around them. Jack in particular was sizing up the dark-haired beauties who crowded the narrow, but often filthy, cobbled streets. "Hey! There Wilky," he cried, "look to that big 'un there. How'd you like to grab that fine sow by the ears?"

"Ho! Jack, me boy. You're right there for I missed that one. Halloa, there, me beauty! Harry Wilkins' the name; 'ave a pot of good ale ready by nightfall and I'll show you what a Derbyshire lad can do to that fine figure of yours!"

"Lookit now, Tom," called Dewdrop. "There's a wee one about your size. You could lose her under old Molly's skirts."

"Ay," retorted Tom, "an' get me head broke in again like as not. 'Tis fine for you single lads, but I'm to keep my tail between me legs while that lump o' Dublin lard's around. But there's fair lookin' drink shops I'll be visiting if we so much as get five minutes to stop from this blasted marchin'."

Shops and booths were open and owners shouted at the soldiers to stop and buy. But the sergeants kept them on the move until the dismiss was sounded in a large tented camp on the heights above the town.

The daily routine here was not unlike that in the barracks at home. Intensive training, sorting kit and unloading stores. The difference was in the huge numbers of troops, the comings and goings of whole regiments, the rattle of drums, and the bugles of the riflemen.

Wellington's allied army was on the move in Central Portugal and his advanced troops had again crossed the frontier into Spain, pursuing the retreating French and keeping up a constant pressure.

On parade one morning, the draft from the 52nd was told it would be moving with many other such reinforcements. They were light infantry and would be joining the famous Light Division under General Robert Crauford – one of the toughest, most stern, yet beloved men who ever led troops in the Peninsular. They were told to be ready to move at daybreak next morning; the rest of the day was their own.

Tom Eagan had his party organised in no time. "Let's be off to the town," he said. "We'll get some food and drink inside of us, for we niver know what terrible things we shall be doing when we start this fighting business!"

They clattered off into the main streets of Lisbon like boys at a fair, laughing, shouting and ready for anything. Molly and some of the wives tagged along for, as she said, "…I'm not going to be missing any fun that's going."

Sally Kinchin joined them, but a certain coolness had developed between her and Jack. Ugly rumours had reached the ears of her corporal and Jack had expressed no desire to continue their assignations if the price of a brief interlude meant twenty lashes from her man or his sergeant.

On the way into the town they came on a large stone-built monastery, now converted into a military hospital. It was a sobering sight for troops who had never seen action. Bullock carts lumbered in and out of the great courtyard, laden with wounded men who had made a journey that had taken days to bring them to this rough and ready place of healing. Some looked far gone and had the colour of death on their faces, but others propped themselves on elbows and shouted crude remarks to the clean and neatly dressed recruits. "Halloa, there boys!" shouted a veteran of the 95th, his dark uniform in rags, and head and arms in dirty bandages. "Look to the Johnny Newcomes, bright lads from old England come to help us out! Get back, lads, get back on a boat while you can. You'll wish you'd never joined when you see them Frenchies coming at you!" He waved his tattered bandages and disappeared under the arch of the main gateway.

Curiosity led the small band of revellers to look into the main courtyard of the hospital. A few orderlies were unloading the wounded, many of whom had received rough surgical treatment in the temporary casualty stations nearer the fighting. The noise from the open windows made the place sound like bedlam and Jack said, "Come on, let's get on our way. This is no place for me."

As he spoke, a soldier called across to them from an open doorway. He was tall, wiry and very sunburned. His uniform was in rags, but as they walked over to join him they saw the few remaining buttons on his jacket were the same as their own. He leant on a crutch, for his left leg stopped short in a sewn-up trouser leg just below the knee.

"New boys, eh?" he asked; "New boys for the old 52nd. Now would one of you fine lads have any baccy on you and maybe a drop of something to cheer up an old soldier down on his luck?"

They crowded round and Jack produced a tobacco tin with some ship's twist inside. Tom slipped a small bottle of rum from his pocket. "Here, soldier, I always has a drop on me in case times is hard and reckon they're hard enough for you."

The wounded infantryman took a long drink, coughed violently and wiped his mouth with the back of his hand. "Thank you, boys. That did me a power of good." Tom indicated he could keep the bottle and the soldier took another swig.

"Where were you wounded?" asked Jack.

"I got it at a place they call Coimbra—only last month, but it seems a year back. It was that blasted mud. Rained for days it did, never saw such rain even during last winter. We was struggling up a hill, slipping and sliding like the pack mules and the French set their cannon on us. Couldn't get away quick enough, ye see. Bang! Down I went with Sergeant Tremayne on top of me. Get up, I shouts, you'll have me drowned in this mud. He didn't speak. Couldn't. He was dead, y'see. I never felt a thing, 'til I rolled the sergeant off me and tried to get up. Me poor old leg was all smashed. One of me mates got me on his back—strong as a lion he was—and slung me on a bullock cart in the rear. The surgeon had me leg off that night and I ended up here."

He spoke with some feeling, for this was the first interested audience he had met. In the hospital nobody wanted to listen to battlefield stories; they all had their own. But the new, enquiring faces had acted as a tonic to him.

"Will ye be going home now, soldier?" asked George Bates.

"Ay, home to old England and ninepence a day pension. They're getting us down to the harbour this week if the transports come."

Billy asked if the veteran had any tips for such new recruits as they.

The wounded man laughed. "Tips? Ay! I'll give you tips. Specially as you're going to the Light Division and you'll be on the move and always up there banging away at old trousers! Damme, what can I tell you?—except to keep your canteen filled with something stronger than water. I had a way with the sergeant as kept the rum kettle and I reckon it was that what kept me going half the time."

Tom Eagan nodded in approval. "Now that sounds a most sensible thing, it does."

"Get some spare stockings," went on the veteran. "Good woollen ones and rub them well with damp soap. You'll march a thousand miles if you can change your socks often enough."

They took it all in, but the atmosphere had changed from the spirited enthusiasm that had started their trip into Lisbon.

"Come on," said Wilkins, "let's get to these taverns and palaces and things you was all so keen about. I've a great thirst on me."

They said farewell to the wounded man who watched them straggling down the hill into the town. He had the look of great experience in the presence of innocence. He had no desire to be with them, knowing that their period of laughter was going to be short-lived.

Soldiers from every regiment and not a few other countries swarmed everywhere in the town. As the fighting moved further away, the Portuguese gave themselves over to providing the rear echelons of the army with every desired comfort. At the same time they were all managing to make their fortunes.

The shopkeepers stood behind their counters while members of their families, preferably attractive daughters, screeched and shouted to the passing troops to "Buy! Buy! Buy!"—buy salami sausage, shoes, trinkets, gewgaws, tin cooking pots, cloth, ladies' wigs, saddles and bridles, hunting dogs and china ornaments. Buy anything! Buy everything! If a greenhorn paused on his bewildered journey, he was whisked inside and relieved of his money before he knew what was afoot.

Tom Eagan steered his party carefully but firmly past all these temptations. He had an instinctive nose for a drink and good company and saw little point in wasting valuable time and even more valuable money on rubbish.

As they strolled down one of the main streets they found themselves approaching a growing sound of voices, smashing glasses and even gunfire. Eagan's eyes lit up. "Oi think t's a fight up ahead!" he cried and quickened his pace.

The end of the street was blocked by a heaving mass of British, German and Portuguese troops, all engaged in a battle royal. In the middle, some shopkeepers and tavern potmen were trying to eject a half dozen Irish soldiers from the considerably damaged front of a wine shop. The Portuguese levies had immediately taken the side of their fellow countrymen and it was only the arrival of a Provost Squad, firing their muskets in the air, that looked like restoring order.

A huge laughing dragoon heaved himself out of the mêlée and dusted down his colourful uniform in front of the party of newcomers. "What's afoot?" asked Jack of the dragoon. "Buttons," said the cavalryman. "Buttons as ever; the same old problem, for the boys will never learn. You can get away with it in the villages, but they're too fly in a place like Lisbon."

Jack looked as puzzled as his comrades. "How come buttons cause a fight like that?"

"Well you *are* new boys, and no mistake," said the dragoon. Eager to show off his knowledge, he explained the reason for the riot. "The boys get short of money very quick in the town, specially the Irish lads with all this liquor around for sale. So they get some spare uniform buttons, hammer them flat on a stone and they look remarkably like a gold dollar, if you pass them quick enough. See what I mean?" He went on his way, laughing.

"Now that's very interesting," said Tom. "Very interesting. I've heard of a few tricks in my time, but that's a beauty and no mistake!" He chuckled at the thought and had already tucked the idea away in his mind to add to the store of devices he had so often employed in his own searches for free drinking.

With the battle of the buttons now under control, they turned off into another street and were soon attracted by the sound of twanging guitars, the beat of tambourines and the welcoming noise of glasses clinking.

"This is it," said Tom and led the way through a high-arched doorway down a flight of stone stairs.

Although it was still the broad daylight of mid-morning, the huge cellar was lit entirely by candles and oil lamps. Racks on both sides supported great barrels of wine and the smaller brandy casks were wedged in between. Heavy oak tables and benches were covered with pewter drinking pots and thin-stemmed glasses. The place was crowded, even for the time of day; yet, so vast was the cavern, a regiment could have taken up quarters there. Waiters and flashing-eyed girls moved around serving drinks and carrying in large wooden trays filled with hot salt beef, garlic and onions, sweetmeats and piles of fresh fruit.

There was shouting and singing, argument and discussion. Some sat back and smoked a pipe with a brandy glass in their hands, content to watch the fun around them. Jack, Tom and the rest, with their womenfolk close behind, were getting their eyesight accustomed to the smoky gloom and moved down the centre of the room to the far end where the music was the main attraction.

Seeing new customers, a waiter heaved a couple of sleeping soldiers on to some sacks in a corner and in no time cleared a table for them. Jugs of wine were brought and the company settled down to take stock of the situation. On a raised platform, a small party of local musicians was quietly playing the soulful and emotive music of Iberia – rich guitar sound and the rhythmic beat of drum and tambourine.

Gulping down the cool wine, lighting pipes and peering around in the gloom, the party became quiet – almost melancholy for a band of soldiers on the eve of their first march towards the enemy.

A young woman had been collecting mugs and wine bottles in the background—a vague, shadowy figure. There was an occasional swish of a skirt, a peal of laughter, a white face revealed under a toss of jet black hair. The candlelight was dim in the recesses of the cellar and only around the musicians' platform was there more light from a ring of large oil lanterns.

One of the musicians called across to the woman in the shadows. "Rosa—Volera, si?" The one word rang back from the girl—"Si!"

Immediately the drum took on a steady beat and one of the guitarists took up a small pipe to give a high, fluting partnership to the drum. The young woman set down her mugs on a table, took a leap to a chair and bounded on to the platform with a flourish that made the candles flicker. From the crowd of soldiers, who obviously knew what was coming next, came a throaty roar of the one word—"Volera!"

She turned slowly to face her audience and, equally slowly, twined her hands together above her head. The women of the Peninsular were dark of hair and skin alike. Yet the black hair of this beauty fell down on to white shoulders and surrounded a full, beautifully proportioned face with large eyes, proud Castilian nose and richly formed lips. A black, low-cut bodice set off in further contrast the whiteness of her skin. The short skirt was flared by a number of coloured petticoats and her feet seemed bare until one noticed the single cords holding flat wooden sandals in the Roman style.

The first loud clash of those sandals on the wooden platform started the tight and formal pattern of the dance. Tiny castanets in each hand played counterpoint to the clacking feet. She swayed and twisted, whirled and spun with a steadily mounting tempo in this, the most abandoned of Portuguese and Spanish dances.

Tom Eagan, in spite of the distraction of Molly busily sucking grapes in the background, was murmuring that he had not seen the like of this before—"…no, not even in Dublin." The others stared in opened-mouthed pleasure.

Jack was sitting as still as a statue, pipe out and a fresh mug of wine untouched. If he was going to maintain that reputation of his, then here was the berth for him. Rough and tumbles in hayfields, sneaking up backstairs in servants' quarters, even the occasional excursion into higher-born boudoirs, somehow paled beside what this sophisticated and sensuous beauty promised.

The dance reached a climax of stamping and clicking, whirling high flying skirts, and a kaleidoscope of black and white flashes. A great roar of approval drowned the final notes and dozens of pewter mugs were thundered on the bare boards. With a triumphant flourish the girl Rosa leaped from the platform and landed neatly among the litter of pots on Jack's table. Pandemonium broke out as soldiers surged forward, throwing coins and shouting their applause.

The lucky party of new soldiers closed ranks to a man, determined to hold this rare and lovely prize.

George Bates took her hand and helped her to a chair between himself and Jack. Brandy was ordered and all turned to Rosa, the champion of the Volera.

Taking a drink of brandy that was thrust upon her, she turned, smiling, and spoke in clear but heavily accented words.

"You new soldiers, eh! Very clean men, new Inglesi soldiers?"

"Glory to God, she speaks English!" cried Tom.

"Where did you learn English?" asked Jack.

"From the soldiers. I been in Lisbon two years. Many Inglesi soldiers in Lisbon all that time." She turned and smiled at Jack who gulped down half a mug of brandy, thinking it was wine. "By the Devil," he said, "this is the finest wench I ever set eyes on. They never looked like this in my village, nor yet in Dorchester either."

"They never danced like that in Dorchester," added his companion.

Jack leant across and spoke quietly to the girl. "Where do you come from, Rosa?"

"You mean where is my home? I come from Albergaria, north from Lisbon, two days by foot, you know. Maybe one day by horse. In Portugal—not Spain—I am Portuguese—father Portugal, mother Spain. Father is shoemaker." She concluded this little speech with a provocative grin of pleasure at her skill in speaking English.

"A shoemaker, eh!" said Jack. "Now there's a thing. I'm a shoemaker too. Perhaps your father and me should get together, like; maybe we could set up shop."

She looked sad for a moment. My father and mother go back to Albergaria after fighting finish there. Many house broken, but our house only a little broken. I will not go back. Have food, drink, many good things here in Lisbon."

Jack had edged his chair closer to the girl and was obviously monopolising her attentions. Slightly fuddled by the drink he was murmuring her name—"Rosa Silvero—Rosa Silvero." He took her slim hand into his. She let out a peal of laughter and cried, "I think this one like me—he like me very much!"

Tom roared at this. "Jack, me boyo, I thought you was goin' off the women these last few days, but I see what you've been saving yourself for. My eyes, but she's a beauty. For myself, of course…" He was interrupted by an argument that had developed around the table about ordering some food. His wife and her companion, Mrs Dawlish, were demanding to be fed.

"Leave them lovebirds alone Tom and keep your eyes off that dark-haired Spanish bitch. I wants me dinner 'fore I starves to a skelington!"

There was a general movement at one end of the table to get some food and more wine sorted out. Only Dick Dewdrop did not join them. He shouted "Hey, Jack lad! Tom's right y'know. She's a beauty and no featherin'. How's about equal shares, you and me?"

Rosa began to protest. "No! I am no cheap soldier's woman…" Jack cut in at once, turning to Dick and grabbing him by the front of his jacket so that the little man was lifted out of his seat.

"I'll see you in Hell first, Dick Dewdrop! I've staked my claim here and I'll fight this whole roomful for her. Go and get one of them big whores over against that wall there. Better still, here's a dollar, Dicky, my little runt. Buy youself a pot of brandy and that'll keep you quiet."

The little man shook himself as Jack pushed him to the end of the table. His muttering changed to a grin as Jack tossed him the coin and he was in the middle of the rest of the crowd, yelling for attention from the waiters.

Jack turned again to Rosa. "Now don't you worry about a thing. I'll protect you from these flea-bitten redcoats."

She flashed a wide smile at him and moved closer to his chair. "I don't worry, Jacko. I know soldiers. They all want to get to my bed. I make friends who I want, not any old soldier."

"That's my girl," said Jack. "You stick by Jack Wheeler and you'll come to no harm. Now would you eat some food with me?"

"No, Jack. No food 'til tonight. I have more dancing to do. Master at this Bodega pay me to dance for soldiers. I like to dance, so everybody happy, yes?"

"Yes, Rosa. Everybody happy. But it's not yet twelve of the clock, so how about you showing me your little room and some of the pretty things I'll wager you've got? You have got a room in the town, haven't you? You don't sleep at this place?"

"No, I don't sleep here. I got a little room. All my own."

"Well that's just fine," he said, looking very relieved. "How about me paying you a call after I've had a bite to eat?"

She laughed quietly and stroked his face. "Go back to camp after I dance, when you hear the drums beat," she said. "Then, perhaps you come later. My room is in this street—you know, by the fountain—over the

wig maker's shop. Now I make ready for the dance."
She looked at him with the most coquettish smile he
had ever seen.

He made one more bid. "In one hour?"

She smiled again. "No. Tonight." She swung from
the table and left Jack with a huge grin on his sweating
face.

He drained his glass, put on his cap and walked
away through the crowded tables. He ignored a shout
from his group, who were now busily eating and
settling down for the day.

From the semi-darkness of the wine cellar he
walked out into brilliant sunshine. Blinking and
staring at the noisy Lisbon scene, he made his way
up the hill to the military camp. He went over to his
tent and flopped down on the straw mattress. For the
rest of the day he slept peacefully.

He was woken by the sharp notes of the bugles
from the Riflemens' Lines. The tent was empty save
for one young soldier laboriously writing a letter
home. The youngster sat on a pile of kit and looked
up as Jack stirred. He grinned shyly and asked, "Had
a good sleep?"

"I have that, lad. Did you not go into the town?"

"No. For I've been writing to my mother all this
afternoon. I'm not a great hand with my letters, but
we march tomorrow and I may never write again if
we are to be in battle soon."

Jack stretched and got up from his mattress.
"That's no way to talk," he said; "The old soldiers say
'tis always their comrade who gets a Frenchman's
bullet, never themselves. Anyway, we're not there yet
and Sergeant Hooper says if you keep your head down
and hold your fire there's no harm can come to you."

The young soldier seemed pre-occupied with his own thoughts so Jack went out of the tent to the water barrel, for he had a burning thirst from the morning's drinking.

In the camp the activity had reached a fever pitch, in spite of the number of men in the town. Bullock carts and pack mules stood in long lines with their loads near completion. The riflemen, whose bugles had just sounded, were mounting the evening guard with noisy ceremonial. Officers were coming from their tents in splendid uniforms and gathering at their central mess for regimental dinners. Smoke poured from a dozen cooking areas.

Jack took a tin bowl of water, washed and shaved carefully, and brushed down his uniform. With the night sky darkening at the approach of sundown, he set out again, down the road into the town.

He walked with a steady, purposeful stride, thinking of the dark-haired Rosa who had made such an impression on him that morning in the wine cellar. As he came nearer to his rendezvous at the Bodega, he noticed more and more soldiers, many of them sleeping soundly in doorways and courtyards. A day spent with unfamiliar wine and raw brandy had produced inevitable results. Jack thought of the state some would be in when it came to the long march in the morning.

Turning a corner he came upon a small group of redcoats dancing down the street to a single fife and followed by a grubby cloud of ragged children. He recognised most of his own group with whom he had spent the morning and was not surprised to see Tom in the centre, coat torn and hat triumphantly waved aloft on a broomstick. They passed without sign of recognition.

Descending the steps into the wine cellar, he was surprised to find how quiet it was down there. In the gloom of the great, low ceilinged tavern, the candles flickered on rows of unoccupied tables. Here and there huddled groups slept with heads buried in folded arms while waiters tidied up in the background. The musicians had gone, but one young guitarist sat in a corner by the platform and picked out a quiet and mournful melody.

He groped his way to a table in one of the many alcoves and picked up a candle to give himself more light. Ordering a glass of wine, he asked the waiter if Rosa was about yet.

The waiter spoke in the halting English of the Lisbonese. "She sleep now, dance later when soldiers come." A silver coin changed hands and the waiter winked solemnly. "I think she wake soon," he said, going off through the beaded curtains.

A few minutes later the curtains parted and the dark-haired beauty came striding towards the alcove, running her hand through her hair and blinking away sleep from her eyes. She sat down and smiled.

"I said I would come," said Jack.

"So, you come to see your Rosa. Many soldiers say they come back, many soldiers do not come back."

Jack ordered wine for her and they drank together without a word.

He remarked how quiet it was. She looked around and nodded. "Oh! Soon many soldiers will come, much drinking, singing, dancing. Always is quiet this time—daytime soldiers come—night-time soldiers come. Now it's twilight, yes? Everybody rests for a big night. Tomorrow the soldiers go—then more come. It is always like this."

Jack thought about the transient nature of military towns, the constant changing faces; the impermanence of everything seemed to sadden him. But he brightened up at the thought of the young woman by his side.

He took one of her hands and stroked it slowly. She moved closer to him. "You're a fine looking girl, Rosa." he said.

She smiled at him and groped for words in his own language. "I think—I think I like you, Jack." She ran a hand across his face. "You're clean man, smooth. Many soldiers are rough, they smell much. You're very clean."

He put an arm around her and pulled her warm, soft body to him. She grinned and slowly swung her head to right and left, brushing his whole face with her long hair. As they moved naturally into a closer embrace his jacket knocked the candle over and it spluttered out in a pool of wine on the table. Nobody noticed.

He kissed her fiercely and smelt a heavy musk-like perfume in her hair. He whispered a request for a quiet rendezvous with her. She pulled away for a moment. With a lightning kiss on his sweating forehead she was away and through the beaded curtain.

Jack sat staring for a long time until disturbed by waiters lighting more candles, the hanging oil lanterns and finding places for the early customers.

He sat there the whole evening, now surrounded by a great roaring, sweating crowd of troops in every kind of uniform. Food was brought and the wine flowed.

Tom, Wilkins and Bates looked in with others from the 52nd draft and joined him. Jack had whispered a few words to Tom and the Irishman led his companions to another corner. "Come on, me lads," he said; "Old Jack's got a shine on for that bit of dancing skirt, so let's not get in his way."

A little after nine o'clock Rosa appeared on the platform to the shouts and cheers of the wine-filled redcoats. She danced a short, spirited fandango and when they roared for more she suddenly held up her hand for silence. A word to the leading guitarist and she went into the stylised movement of a sultry yet rhythmical bolero. Several times her flashing eyes were on the silent figure in the alcove.

The food and drink came in ever-increasing quantities and all manner of impromptu pieces of skylarking broke out. For her last appearance that evening, Rosa gave her audience the Volero, that wild and uninhibited display that had so intrigued Jack that morning. The troops went mad as the fife and tabor played faster and louder, while Rosa's stamping feet moved like flashes of lightning. Her final flourish went beyond that of the morning, for she leapt from table to table around the entire area of the platform, scattering tankards, mugs, soldiers' hats and not a few of the soldiers themselves.

Jack half rose from his chair as he saw her leaping towards his table. With a swish of skirts she was in front of him for barely a second and then off across the room. But a metallic clang in the pewter mug before him made him start like a rabbit. The others around him were leaping about and standing on chairs to yell their encouragement of the dancer, so nobody noticed him fish the large iron door key from the wine mug and slip it into his pocket.

A different sound now vied with the local music – a military drum beating the army's oldest call – a tattoo. This signal penetrated the minds of all but the very drunk and with much shuffling, last minute draining of pots, and straightening of uniforms, the troops began to move towards the main door.

Jack took a last look at the curtain through which his Rosa had disappeared and set out himself. A provost sergeant and ten men of the town guard strode in and began marshalling the more reluctant soldiers.

"Come now, you rascals!" he shouted. "Let's see you on the road to camp. Let's have you on your feet for you've to be up at daybreak and a right long march ahead of you!"

Jack elbowed his way to the street and the cool night air. He set out quickly for the camp, occasionally patting the iron key in his pocket and thinking with excitement of new adventures before the sun rose and the long march began.

At the camp the last of the stores had been loaded. Candles flickered in the long lines of tents and a blaze of light came from the officers' quarters where some sort of ball appeared to be in progress.

Soldiers lurched and staggered all over the place and there was a good deal of noise as the more lively were bedded down by their comrades.

In his own tent, Jack removed his shoes and jacket, rolled himself in his blanket and soon appeared to be asleep. Most of the occupants were settling down and the complement of the tent was completed when three men staggered in with a now silent form of Tom Eagan. There was a little shuffling and muttering such as, "Get his jacket off for mercy's sake—here, I have one of his shoes—mind his head the poor ould cratur—by the Lord he's taken a load on tonight!"

The head of Sergeant Hooper was thrust through the tent flap and by the light of an oil lantern he counted his charges. "Sweet dreams, my bonny boys. I'll be rousing you in the morning." He blew out their candle stuck in an upturned bayonet and the tent was given over to heavy snores and drunken grunts.

Jack lay still and quiet for almost an hour. The sounds from the officers' mess showed no signs of abating, but the rest of the camp was comparatively quiet. He rose, slipped on his shoes and jacket and crept silently out into a clear, moonlit night. Moving swiftly in the direction of a hedge, he showed all the countryman's skill of night manoeuvre. He worked his way along the tightly grown base of the hedge until he found what he wanted; a small gap that had obviously been used for this same purpose by others before him. He was through, then loping swiftly down the road, ears and eyes alert, and ready to move into the shadows if accosted.

In the town there were still odd parties of soldiers and civilians roaming about, but in most places the inhabitants were asleep behind closely shuttered windows. He gained the street that was now becoming familiar to him and moved on to the fountain at the end. An oil lamp burned nearby and he looked around the tops of the row of shops until he could make out the distinct outline of a wig maker's sign. This was it and he was through the courtyard at the side and up a narrow flight of wooden stairs in a matter of seconds.

The first floor landing was not entirely dark, for a tiny flame burned in front of a religious statue. Jack felt grateful for even this small light, but his heart beat fast when he noticed two doors in front of him as well as the stairs leading up to a further part of the house.

"The Devil have me for a fool. Which one did she mean?"

He stood quite still for a while and then thought he'd come so far not to be put off by further risks. He moved silently to the right hand door and with great care slipped the key into the lock and turned slowly. It creaked a bit for want of oil, but the lock gave and he peered into the gloom. Another light, this time by a Saint's picture, made him sigh with relief. He looked into the empty room and strongly approved of this business of burning night lights.

He slipped into the room and closed the door. He noticed the window was curtained inside and shuttered on the outside, so he took a stump of candle from his pocket and, begging the Saint's pardon, lit it from the tiny oil lamp and stuck it on a small table.

A glance showed him it was Rosa's room all right. A tambourine and some castanets on the table gave him his first clue he was in the right place and a small wooden trinket box with the name **ROSA** neatly burned on the lid made him smile to himself that all was now well.

He hung his jacket on a chair and slipped off his shoes. "Might as well be comfortable," he thought. He stretched out on the small wooden bed and laid his head on a lace-worked pillow. Everything was neat and very clean.

His Dorset village was hundreds of miles away and he had left it in search of adventure. Well, he thought, this was as good a start as any.

He lay for some time with his thoughts and was just considering getting a pipe of tobacco going when soft footsteps were heard on the creaking stairs and landing. He held his breath as the door slowly opened and that lovely white face looked into the room.

She smiled in greeting and put a finger to her lips for silence. She seemed to glide into the room as though in the slow movement of one of her dances - a slim, beautiful and wholly desirable young woman.

Jack swung off the bed and leaned back against the wall for a moment to take a good look at her. Again she cautioned silence as he made a move towards her; she held up her hand in a gesture that clearly said, "Patience!" His own clothes were an untidy heap on the floor in a matter of seconds.

He returned to the bed and she sat at her small table and carried out an elaborate and feminine ritual of her toilet. Large earrings, the theatrical rings and other jewellery were all carefully removed and put away in the trinket box. Hair was brushed and water poured in a small basin for washing.

Jack fidgeted with ill concealed excitement and impatience. Suddenly she turned, smiled and blew out the candle. There was a swirl of silk as her dress was removed and a few seconds later Jack felt the girl's warm breath on his face and this fine young woman was beside him.

His broad arm seemed to engulf her as she wriggled around in the bed. He showered impatient kisses around her face and neck. He was aware of some rich-smelling oil or scent which she had spread over her body. They came to their ultimate embrace in a few minutes. The temperature rose on a spring night in Lisbon.

The banging of some shutters and the barking of a dog penetrated the depth of Jack's sleep. He stirred and without waking Rosa, crept from the bed, pulled aside the curtains and pushed open one of the shuttered windows. Streaks of light gave a pink tone to the misty morning.

He stood looking out into the gathering light, then turned to watch the face in its framework of black hair on the lace trimmed pillow. He felt an infinite and resigned sadness that he was already caught in a huge machine; already committed to leave hurriedly and go about a strange and new business – the very business that had brought him to this foreign country.

Time was short and he had no wish to start his active service life with a flogging. Desertion, he knew, was punishable by death and in spite of his new and affectionate attachment to the sleeping girl, he realised his wild thoughts of the previous evening were hopeless ones. He had changed his village and parents for the comradeship and promised adventures of a soldier's life. Rosa seemed part of this adventure and gave meaning to it all. He now felt he had a stake in the Peninsular.

He dressed quickly and splashed some cold water over his face. Sitting on the side of the bed, he stroked the forehead of the girl until she opened her eyes with a start. She smiled, then frowned as the fully dressed soldier at her side reminded her that today he marched north to find the war. She pulled him down to her and they whispered, hurriedly and with the minimum of words. Would he see her again? Did he want to see her again? Would she remember him? Of course! Of course! The old phrases that never changed when lovers parted after a night such as this.

Jack straightened up and held her hand for one more brief moment. Then with a turn he was out of the door and down the stairs. She leaped from the bed and was leaning from the window before he had gained the street outside. She turned to her table and grabbed the first thing that came to hand on the top of the trinket box. It was a silver locket on a chain and one of her large red earrings had become caught up with it. She called softly to the soldier who involuntarily looked up at her window.

"Come back to me—come back soon."

She threw the memento and he caught it in one hand. He looked at the two trinkets and then gave her a last wave. It was now full light and even at this distance the bugles could be heard at the camp on the hill. He set off up the street at his loping run, jumping from side to side to avoid the piles of rubbish and peering quickly round corners to see that no military authority was out rounding up stragglers.

In spite of the unknown that lay ahead, he felt like shouting with sheer high spirits. He was a happy man.

Chapter Four

Hold Your Fire

As Jack approached the camp, a nagging fear grew that his name might already be posted as missing. There was a rising tide of sound from the top of the hill; a sound made by an army very much awake and getting ready for the road.

Slipping through the hole in the hedge, he was not noticed in the great confusion of men hurrying to and fro, most burdened with piles of stores and equipment. He went straight to his tent where he found Sergeant Hooper getting Tom Eagan and the other revellers of the previous night on to their feet and in a reasonable condition for parade. Jack was hurriedly packing his kit and rolling his blanket when Hooper noticed him.

"Where the devil have you been, Wheeler?"

"Moving officers' stores," replied Jack, in a flash of inspiration.

"I don't recall marking you for that duty. Get yourself outside and take charge of this Irish friend of yours. I've a notion someone will be carrying him before the morning is through and it won't be me!"

Hooper left the tent and Jack went over to Tom to help him with the straps of his knapsack.

"Oh, Jack me boy," moaned the Irishman, "I've a head on me like Mother Kelly's soup pot. I don't think I could march this day. Tell the Gineral I'll be joining him in the fight tomorrow. Where's me musket? Who's thieved me musket?"

They moved out into the great field where already the lines of mule and bullock-drawn baggage trains were rumbling off. Portuguese drivers cracked long-hide whips and urged the beasts on with guttural shouts.

The drafts were forming up in regiments, long lines of men in ranks of fours with drums and fifes at the head of each column. There were no colours, for these would be met when the reinforcements joined the main army. But an officer rode at the head of each draft and others were placed at intervals along the line of march.

Hooper marshalled his group with care and skilfully checked each man's equipment. There was a moment of cheering when that part of the baggage train moved past where the soldiers' wives had placed themselves. Some of the women were perched on high at the top of the piles of baggage on the huge wagons, but Molly Eagan was astride a newly acquired donkey that had already been named "The Queen of Spain".

She shouted across to her husband. "Tom, Tom, we're goin' to the fight—the women'll have finished off them Frenchies 'fore you get your musket loaded. Oi'll have a drop of tea for youse all in the first bivyack and mind you have a taste of rum for me!" She shrieked with laughter as the overloaded donkey lurched through the gateway and on to the road.

The Rifles moved out with their light, easy step, every man a combatant including the young buglers. Then came shouts of, "Look to your front, 52nd. Fall out, officers—sergeants, to your men!" The now familiar rattle of drums and shrilling of pipes set backs a little straighter and heads high. In warm sunshine they marched through the gateway and were soon passing their own baggage wagons on the road to the Peninsular War.

The roads of Portugal were little more than rock-strewn tracks with frequent potholes; but British troops had been tramping them for years now and the new soldiers soon had the knack of avoiding the flints and mud patches. They swung along to the sound of the drum and a good deal of coarse singing.

Tom was looking pale and after the first hour complained of feeling dizzy. Jack took his musket from him to help his friend and they tramped on together. At midday they were halted and the order came down the line to pile arms and make a quick meal. A few started preparing fires, but the sergeants pointed out that there was no time for such luxuries. "Fires tonight, my lads and a bit of roast beef for your bellies," said Sergeant Hooper. "Biscuits and water are all we've time for now, as I hear Lord Wellington is waiting for us."

Tom Eagan had brightened up now as his mammoth hangover declined. He squatted down beside Jack and munched biscuits. "Would youse like a pull from me canteen, Jacko? It's a better flavour than that mouldy water you're drinking."

Jack took the round wooden water canteen, pulled the cork and scented the pungent red wine smell before he had the canteen to his lips. He took a good swig.

"You're a man to soldier with, Tom. You promised we'd not go short of anything."

"Ay! We'll do our bit, sure enough," said Tom.

They were urged to their feet by the rolling drums and the shouts of the sergeants. On they went down the road bordered by fresh spring flowers and past fields of young wheat. From vegetable patches and olive groves the peasants looked up from the work and waved. They crossed themselves for the soldiers going to war and in hopes that the fire and fury of battle would not come into their locality.

The sergeants had been considerate of the draft on their first long march and had not forced the pace. The bivouac for the night was a sloping field with many young trees and a stream at the bottom. The men eased their heavy knapsacks from aching shoulders, laid out their bed spaces and set about making themselves comfortable. In little groups they gathered dead wood and had fires going by the time the first of the baggage and commissariat wagons arrived.

Each soldier carried iron rations for seven days, mainly consisting of dried salt beef or goats' meat and large flat biscuits. These were meant for the midday meal and such times as the line of march was detached from the main supply column. The experienced troops always kept a day's hard tack in hand for the food situation was one of the most hazardous of the campaign. As soon as troops were near to the battle line, there was a normal issue of a litre of wine a day, if the commissariat drivers had not sold or drunk it en route.

That night was like a country picnic, with the fires burning well and cook-pots of beef and vegetable stew on the boil. Each small group of men selected a tree and hung their knapsacks, canteens and other equipment from the branches. After food and a pipe they rolled in their blankets and greatcoats, lay down under the stars and the dark shapes of the trees.

The married men crept quietly up to the line of wagons on the road and made little bedrooms under the high wheeled carts. Molly Eagan, who had already acquired a store of spare blankets and canvas sheets, had draped an ox cart until it resembled a gypsy caravan. The sergeant of the guard, making his night rounds with a corporal, noticed this cosy cave with a candle burning inside. "You'll have to get this lot packed in double-time tomorrow, Mrs Eagan," he called as he passed. He was answered by a well aimed boot from the lady herself.

He laughed and turned to his corporal. "We've a right handful with that one, I'm thinking. Reckon his Lordship's whole Provost Corps couldn't handle her if it came to a fight."

The days passed pleasantly and almost without noticing it the rate of march was being increased. Twenty miles the first day, then twenty-five, twenty-eight and now thirty miles from sunrise to sunset. The troops had outstripped their baggage train and a good deal of foraging began for the nightly meal.

Tom Eagan and a few of his Irish comrades were experts at this and as they passed through a village the clucking of hens and geese meant poultry for dinner that night. The bayonet proved a universal tool, for it dug raw vegetables out of the ground and acted as a spit for roasting a hare or chicken.

Until now the reinforcements had marched north, but on reaching the town of Leiria the line turned east and headed for the frontier into Spain.

Leiria brought the new troops face to face with some of the harsher realities of war. The French had always lived off the country, whether in advance or retreat. In retreat they were merciless as they swept through a town or village, stripping it of everything edible. With the Allies under Wellington pressing hard on their heels in the Spring of 1811, they still paused for vengeance on the Portuguese whose troops were marching with the British and whose guerrillas would creep into the French lines at night to write off old scores with the knife. When a town like Leiria lay in the path of the French, it was soon reduced to a holocaust of fire and brutal murder.

Much had been cleared up when the spruce new columns marched through, but the smell of burning, the doors torn from hinges, the smashed furniture in the street, and the unburied human and animal dead that cluttered the alleyways had a sobering effect on the new boys.

This stark picture also had the effect of quickening the steps of the troops who were now eager to make their own retribution for what they had seen. As the grim-faced men marched out of this devastated town, they came upon little groups of people, mainly women and children, who had fled into the countryside and survived the terrible fury of the French. Now they hovered on the outskirts, frightened to move back to their homes; uncertain and without leadership, they stood in ragged clusters and pointed to gaping mouths. Starvation always followed these violent incidents and the hard-driving

British redcoats ignored the warnings of the sergeants and handed out the meagre rations they were supposed to reserve for themselves.

"Ah, well!" shouted one, as he tossed the last of his biscuits to the skeleton of a child. "We'll need to lighten our load if they're going to keep up this pace."

They waded across rivers and worked their way up the mountain passes that brought them gradually nearer to the main army. The weather remained fine and the miles swept by with increasing speed as they moved downhill towards the three river valleys of the Coa, the Jurones and the Dos Casas.

Wellington had halted his army on some high ground overlooking the village of Fuentes de Onoro and waited for the French attack. There was every indication that the French retreat had at last come to a halt and that they were gathering forces to turn and strike back.

A senior staff officer, galloping up to the head of the reinforcement column, brought this news and urged all speed if the new troops were not to be late for their first engagement with the enemy.

Then followed one of those historic marches of the Peninsular, when raw troops with their spirits up crossed nearly fifty miles of rough terrain in twenty-four hours. With short breaks for the minimum of food and drink, they pressed on by moonlight - a sweating, dust grimed column of men. There was little talk or laughter now, only the clinking of arms and the steady tramp of marching feet.

It was a remarkable achievement for men new to the Peninsular, although it did not surpass the now legendary story of a reinforcement draft of the Rifles who marched sixty-two miles in twenty-six hours to arrive on the field of Talavera in the summer of 1809.

The distant rumbling of artillery acted as a spur to the column of men and in the early morning of the 2nd of May they crossed the Coa River and saw the breathtaking sight of an army preparing for battle.

In the few weeks since they had left their homes and taken the shilling, they had become accustomed to the apparent chaos of troops both on the move from barracks in England and at the camp at Lisbon. Here everything seemed to belong, everything worked to an unwritten plan as part of a composite scheme of intense activity.

Whole regiments were moving off the road and deploying in the fields that sloped down to two rivers. The new boys saw for the first time the regimental colours and the British flag carried at the head of each column. They formed up quickly in a field and moved off in drafts to join their regiments, at last a part of an integral body within the army. Jack and Tom, marching together behind Sergeant Hooper, were at the head of their draft and looked about them with excited anticipation at the bivouacked Light Division.

"Here we are, Jack," said Tom, "home at last and me pour ould feet a'killing me. Tell his Lordship to hold off any fighting 'til I've had a bit of a rest and a bite to eat for I'm fair killed already after all that tramping."

They halted and rested on their arms as the officers with the draft went to a group of tents to report their arrival. There was a bustling around the largest tent and grooms brought thoroughbred horses forward. Soon the sunburned figure of General Robert

Crauford appeared with Brigadier Drummond and their ADCs. Mounting, they rode slowly towards the draft who were called to attention and awaited inspection by the legendary commander of the Light Division.

He first rode up and down in front of them, peering down into faces until he noticed Sergeant Hooper. "Hooper, is it not? Good to see you back in Spain. Have you brought me some good 'uns? I don't want any of that old tavern rubbish!"

The sergeant stiffened with pride and grinned up at his old commander. "These are good 'uns Sir. You'll have 'em a credit to the Light Division inside a week."

The General backed his horse a few steps and the troops waited for the inevitable exhortation to do their duty. But Crauford was a man of hard reputation and few words. "I welcome you to my Division. I like the look of you and the march you've just made is evidence that you're the men I need. Lord Wellington had just sent me word that we should be seeing something of the enemy within twenty-four hours or less. Good luck to you!"

The man who had led the Light Division through so many actions in the Peninsular, bringing his men intact through the terrible retreat to Corunna to get them to England, turned his horse and rode off to the army commander's headquarters. Experience and confidence were written on his lined face and he was not among those who had any qualms about the work that had to be done next day.

Drummond, commander of one of the two light infantry brigades, gave a few orders to the new draft and told them how they would be put in with the veterans of their regiment. They were ordered to get food and then rest after their long march to prepare themselves for the now imminent attack expected from over the river on their front.

At the dismiss, the men hurried across to the cook-pots and over beef stew and mugs of the local wine nicknamed "blackstrap", they mingled with their new comrades.

Here there was no ribaldry of comments about the newcomers, although their lighter skins and smarter appearance contrasted with the sun-tanned faces and tattered, faded uniforms of the veterans.

Sergeant Hooper found an old comrade and introduced him to Jack and the boys. The old warrior pointed to the village of Fuentes and said, "See that little lot; reckon we know every street and house down there, for we've fought over it twice before by my calculation. Ay! With you new lot thickening up the squares, we'll give old trousers a drubbing tomorrow, if he chooses to come tipping his hat in this direction."

Throughout the afternoon they slept under hedges and against the walls of the gardens on the outskirts of the village. As night fell and the mists rolled up from the river, the little group of forward sentries moved into their outposts. Most of the baggage wagons and animals had been moved to the rear and those of the new draft were still plodding along the main road over twenty miles back. An occasional braying of a donkey, the barking of a dog, and the quiet movements of the sentries changing stations were the only evidence of a large army at rest on the eve of battle.

It was still quite foggy when first light broke the skyline. The forward sentries were withdrawing and reporting a good deal of activity on the other side of the river. There was little noise from the allied army as it woke, rolled blankets, ate hard tack and stood to arms on the morning of the 3rd of May.

From across the river, bugles grew louder and louder and soon the shouting of NCOs and the jingling of harness could be heard. The moving into position of the seven British and Portuguese Divisions, the Horse Artillery and the clouds of cavalry was carried out with speed, efficiency and remarkably little noise.

Jack, Tom and their comrades from the recruiting march found themselves in the middle of a square facing the northern corner of the village with Portuguese artillery and infantry reserves drawn up on the higher ground to their rear. With a spirited clatter, the riders, guns and limbers of Bull's Troop, Royal Horse Artillery, galloped into position between the redcoat squares and set up shop for the day's business. Round shot, canister and grape were dumped around the guns and the first charges rammed home as the infantry were doing the same with ball and powder cartridge in their muskets.

As the sun rose and the mist lifted, a great panoramic scene appeared on the far bank of the river. French cavalry were wheeling and turning to prepare for a charge. Huge and apparently ill co-ordinated masses of infantry jostled and pushed forward with banners flying, drums beating and bugles joining in the racket. The British squares waited in silence.

By mid-morning, as the rum kettles were going round the Light Division, the French artillery opened up to be answered immediately by Wellington's gunners. Tom Eagan had just put a tin mug full of liquor to his lips when the first crash came and the brown liquid splashed over his face and down the white pipeclay of his cross-straps. "The Devil blast their eyes!" he yelled. "Niver a drop went down at all! I'll have 'em for that, so I will!" He raised his musket to his shoulder but at once the voice of Sergeant Hooper rang out. "Hold your fire, man! It's you, is it, Eagan? I'll have you flogged! You've a while yet, so stand your ground and hold your fire 'til I tell you!"

The cannonade increased in volume and frequency. Twice the French shells found the corner of Jack's square, the first time merely showering them with earth but the second sending a man in the front rank rolling on the ground with an ugly head wound.

"Stand to your places! Hold your fire!" roared Hooper above the din. In a few seconds he had the man over his shoulder, round to the back of the square and saw him carried off to the rear slung in a blanket by two Portuguese muleteers. The front rank closed and continued a tight-lipped, silent staring towards the advancing French cavalry screen and the clouds of French skirmishers.

The noise increased all along the line and the first rattling of Brown Bess muskets firing in unison could be heard to the right where the 3rd Division had made contact. The French cavalry seemed very close now, having splashed across the shallow river and jostled for positions facing the village. Sporadic fire was coming from the advancing clusters of infantry, in spite of the pounding they were getting from Wellington's artillery. A few balls whistled over and around the British squares and the orders rang out from the officers as they galloped to and fro between their lines of men.

"Look to your muskets—fire!" screamed Hooper and a great crash engulfed the waiting men. Smoke enveloped them for a few moments and, as it cleared, they saw the fantastic scene to their front as though an invisible scythe had been at work in a cornfield. A complete area of French cavalry and infantry had been flattened to the width of the British square. Horses and men were rolling about in frantic chaos and not a few would never move again.

The veterans of the 52nd were already on their knees and reloading. "Get down, down, reload!" roared Hooper. As they dropped to their knees a similar crash of musketry came from behind and a shrieking, whistling noise of a hundred bullets passed over their heads. The Portuguese to their rear were working in unison with them. These were the tactics that had made Wellington famous: the steadfast holding of infantry squares, controlled and devastating fire, and the careful placing of his troops to do the maximum damage in the shortest space of time.

After firing their first shot a great tension seemed to ease the men. As they pulled out cartridges and wielded ramrods, they shouted and laughed to each other. Time-honoured, simple sayings of soldiers under fire—"If me old mother could see me now!" "Who'll have a game of dice!" "I'll take me pension and a quart of ale when this day's over!" and many more.

Tom nudged Jack beside him. "Did ye see me fire me musket? Didn't I make a better noise than the time the boys blew up Dublin Castle? That Molly of mine had better have tea ready, for this is warm work."

Within a quarter of a minute the square was ready again with muskets loaded and aimed for fire. The command rang out and another of those deafening crashes rolled round the tightly-packed ranks of the men. Hooper worked his men like a demon, moving among them, urging, cursing, encouraging and turning to his officers as they rode back and forth with fresh orders. Several times he acted on his own, deflecting the concentration of fire slightly to the left or right whenever the French looked like recovering. "To the right a bit, lads! That lot round their colours! Hold it! Fire!"

The new men fell in with the rhythm set by their experienced comrades. Apart from the French artillery there was little return fire and casualties on the British front were light. Once a French rifle bullet thumped into the man on Jack's right as they fired another volley. Even above the crash of their own arms Jack seemed to hear the bullet find its mark and he almost jumped with the man beside him as it happened. The soldier leaned for a second on his musket and stared as though surprised. He made no sound as he crumpled up in a heap at Jack's feet. Frantically reloading, Jack yelled to the fellow, "Are you hit, matey?" The man opened his eyes, put his hand to his chest and promptly fainted again. Hooper was in the ranks in a flash and had the wounded man dragged to the rear as Jack straightened up. Hooper called over his shoulder—"Leave any trouble to me, you keep loading, boys, and never mind the French!"

Once, as the smoke cleared from one of their volleys and they were reloading now with demoniac speed, Jack noticed a tight group of mounted officers riding close to their rear. "Hey! Tom, boys, look now!

That's surely Lord Wellington himself!" The veterans recognised their Commander-in-Chief at once and raised a ragged cheer. Tom Eagan got a laugh by shouting, "God bless you, Sir, an' your old black hat. It's a grand day we're all havin' an' you around to see the play!"

Wellington reined his horse for a moment and turned to Crauford riding beside him. "A good square that, Robert. A good square. New men among them too, I see."

"Thank you, Sir," said Crauford and turned to the men. "Keep 'em at it, Hooper. There's plenty of work to be done yet!"

Hooper grinned with pleasure. He doubled to his place on the right of the square and roared them back to the business in hand. Before Wellington and his Divisional Commander had gone a dozen paces the square had sent another stream of musket balls crashing towards the French lines.

By now the men were blackened with powder and their uniforms stained with sweat. The perspiration ran down inside their shirts and trousers and not a few had their hats off to cool their heads.

The smoke became thicker where the infantry was keeping up the fire and only brief glimpses were now seen of the broken French advance. But Wellington had galloped to the higher ground at the rear and saw, with that rapid way he had, the situation at a glance. The French were so badly mauled that those still on their feet were firing wildly and withdrawing step by step. The cavalry had already pulled back for they were the most vulnerable when the British infantry handed out the treatment of firing by squares.

It was then the British cavalry had the chance for which they had been impatiently waiting all morning. A few quick orders, a galloping to the squadrons by mounted officers and the trumpets sent the dragoons off like huntsmen at a find. At that moment Jack and the boys in the square were told "hold your fire", and they put their hats on the ends of smoking muskets, cheering like schoolboys as the horsemen thundered through. A confused, smoke-ridden chaos seemed to lie ahead, but in the squares discipline was still maintained.

Then the order came down to advance the infantry, not in a charge but steadily and to occupy the whole village and beyond. Bayonets were fixed and the men moved forward at a steady, fast walking pace into the main square of the village and spreading out to the gardens on the far side.

They passed hundreds of dead and dying French troops in their blue uniforms, now looking like broken toys. The living pleaded for help but the 52nd were light infantry and needed in a definite place as part of their Commander's plan. Jack paused to prop a French cavalry officer against the wall of a house and to unstop the man's own canteen and put it to his lips. The officer had a badly shattered arm and his remaining good one was shaking so much he poured the coarse wine everywhere but in his mouth.

"Leave that be!" roared Sergeant Hooper's voice in Jack's ear. "There's plenty to do that job; I've work for you to your front!"

The formation of a square was no longer needed, for they found ample protection behind the walls of gardens, mounds of earth and the piled debris of guns, limbers, ammunition boxes and even dead mules. Jack's group flung themselves down behind a stone wall at the back of a baker's shop. Sergeant Hooper had posted himself in the upstairs room of a house along the street and was recklessly hanging out of the window to call his orders.

"Keep your eyes open and fire in your own time!" he shouted.

"By the crown, I'm as thirsty as old nick. Would anybody have a drop left in his canteen?" asked Jack. The man beside him passed up a few mouthfuls of wine, but already Tom was creeping back into the house and shop behind them. He reappeared clutching a huge lump of damp and very dirty, half-cooked dough that he had rescued from one of the ovens.

"Where's all this loot I heard so much about? That shop's as empty as our regimental drum. Them Frenchies have even taken the curtains from the windows and all I found was this lump of dough. The ovens is cold, so we'll have to warm it up when we get a fire goin'."

The others were making their usual derisory remarks whenever Tom was complaining about his lot, when one of them noticed a bulge in the Irishman's jacket.

"That's not dough you've under your jacket, Tom," he said; "Happen you found a bit of booty after all. Come on, you Irish tinker, let's have a share, whatever it is."

"Sure, wasn't I going to do that very thing. But there's precious little for so many of you and on a day such as this an' all!" He undid the front of his jacket and produced with a flourish a near empty bottle of brandy.

A heavily built ex-coal heaver from Newcastle lunged forward and grabbed the bottle. "Gie it 'ere now, mon, I'm fair shoutin' for a drop!"

There was a general scramble around the few drops of brandy when the eagle eye of Sergeant Hooper spotted them from his window. He roared across the street, "Look to your front, you redcoat swine. By God, Eagan if I catch you at that lark again I'll skin you. Look to your front, they're coming at us!"

They were too; reinforcements and rallied troops had been formed up and were fording the stream at the eastern side of the village. Hooper took over and climbing out on to a roof where he could see most of his men, shouted his commands. By sheer lung power his powerful voice was heard above the racket of this second attack. Each time the men waited until his voice rang out with the single command—"Fire!"

In front of the village the attack was held, but on the left by the open ground the line was giving way and the 52nd were in danger of being cut off. They withdrew through the village street, the rearguard being Hooper's Company. In smashed doorways and debris littered courtyards, Jack and Tom had their first taste of street fighting and much of it was too close to be healthy.

At one point Hooper directed a small group with Jack and Tom to hold a gateway to a courtyard and let a troop of Horse Artillery through. In the clatter and confusion the men turned only just in time to see six tall French dragoons clear the wall at their rear and come at them with sabres swinging.

Tom fired first and had the leader down. The volley from the others brought four more to a thrashing pile of horses and men in the middle of the yard. But one was unhurt and came for the gateway like a fiend out of hell.

Gripping his still smoking and empty musket, Jack had a momentary glimpse of a foam-decked, huge black horse, a shining breastplate and sunlight on a raised sabre. It all happened in three seconds – Jack thrust the long Brown Bess upwards in both hands like a quarter staff and took the shock of the sabre blow as it clanged on the metal of the barrel. Tom swung his weapon from the muzzle end and roared in fury and pain as his hands gripped the still hot barrel and he dealt the rider a blow to the head that sent his gorgeously plumed helmet into the dust and its owner right after it.

Sergeant Hooper had pricked the horse with a bayonet point that sent it careering through the gateway and crashing into a British gun team as they thundered past.

A quick look round, a breathless "Thanks, Tom" from a trembling Jack and they were all off down the road like runners in a marathon.

They reformed into squares, reloaded and stood their ground. But Wellington had held three regiments of one division in reserve and these now charged forward to retake the village and even get across the river on the far side.

The Light Division were ordered at their customary fast pace to help their comrades of the 5th and 6th Divisions at the northern end of the line, but travelling at the double they found the French attack there to be nothing more than a demonstration and were pulled back to the rear as night began to fall.

The French had had more than enough for one day and retreated all along the front in the fading light. Night closed in at Fuentes de Onoro as the Light Division marched wearily up the slope to the bivouac position. Jack trudged along beside Tom, each with his own thoughts. He felt as tired as the rest, yet strangely excited that he had not only survived his first battle but kept his fears to himself and not felt any inclination to cut and run when the action of the day had been at its hottest. He confided his feelings to Tom. "Y'know Tom, I thought I'd be scared as the devil with all that banging and shouting and the French guns slamming away right at us. But you don't seem to think when it's all around you—you just keep at it."

The Irishman grinned and spat on the ground. "I think you're right Jack, me lad, 'tho there was a few times I remembered a prayer me ould mother taught me, for I thought I'd be sleeping under the ground tonight."

"Ah, we'll sleep well tonight, I reckon," said Jack. "They say the Frenchies don't ever attack at night and they'd not get far with that mist coming up from the river."

Their casualties had been remarkably light for a day of heavy fighting, a total of 259 in Wellington's entire army. As the men converged in columns on their assembly areas they passed little groups of supply troops bringing in wounded and in one corner by some trees a burial party was at work.

It was quite dark now and the mist over the river hid the lanterns of the French who had far larger casualties to deal with. A number of poor souls would be overlooked on a night like this and forced to lie wounded in the hope of surviving until dawn.

Over the ridge, the boys came upon the welcome sight of dozens of fires and boiling cook-pots. Tea kettles were on the go everywhere and names being shouted to make up groups for the evening meal together. The draft's baggage train had arrived and there was plenty to eat and drink.

Tom and Jack flung off their equipment by a familiar wagon where Mrs Skilly was standing by a stew-pot with rolled up sleeves and an iron ladle in her hand. "Come on lads!" she called. "Here's a drop of tea and rum and some good pork stew after your hard day's work. Have ye seen that sergeant of mine or has he got 'imself killed already?"

Tom was first at the pot and demanding news of his wife. "Did the fat cow fall off her moke or something? She's niver around when you want her!"

"She was 'ere but an hour since, Tom. Said something about goin' to look for you."

Tom seemed unperturbed, feeling that his wife was indestructible anyway and he slumped down with a bowl of stew against the front wheels of the wagon. Jack joined him and they ate voraciously. They had just got their pipes going and Jack was thinking the scene was not unlike the imaginative dreams of his civilian days when there was a rustling under the high baggage wagon.

A woman's voice whispered just behind them: "Tom, Tom, keep still, man, and don't make a show. Look what ould Molly's brought you."

The two men crawled under the wagon where Molly was crouched, removing an assortment of packages and bundles from her clothing.

"You Clonmel bitch!" hissed Tom. "Where in the name of St Patrick 'ave you been?"

"I've brought you some presents, boys. Reward for your brave fighting today. When the banging of them guns stopped and they all said up here the day's work's over, I went to find you. I got right down by the river and there was all these dead Frenchies around – God rest their souls. Now I figured they wouldn't need ought where they was goin', so I eased 'em out of them great knapsacks they wear and laid 'em out decent like. They keep a rare lot of stuff in them knapsacks."

Tom grinned and gave his wife a resounding slap. "You're a hard woman, Moll, but there's some sense in you for all that. What's the score?"

She had several bottles of brandy, an officer's fine lace shirt and a little pile of gold and silver coins. The loot was divided between them, a brandy bottle went the rounds, and all three snuggled up under their blankets and slept. For a few moments Jack thought wistfully about his Rosa, but fatigue had him snoring with his companions in a matter of a minute.

A little after midnight a bullock broke loose from its cart and blundered into the rows of neatly piled arms in the Light Division's lines. The clatter caused a stampede among some officers' horses and in seconds bugles were sounding the alarm. Sergeants were on their feet shouting hoarsely and the cry was taken up—"Cavalry, French cavalry!"

Jack woke from a deep sleep and violently shook Tom at his side. "Get up Tom! French cavalry in the lines!"

"God rot them," moaned the Irishman. "I'll 'ave their guts for breaking my sleep."

Even Molly seized a loaded musket and made threatening movements by the light of the wagon's lantern. It took half an hour to sort out the chaos. A few more hours of sleep and they were roused again, cursing and groaning at the fact that it was still dark. But Wellington never took chances and had his entire army standing to before dawn broke on another misty morning.

The mist hung about for some hours after the sun had risen and on the other side of the river the French continued picking up wounded and burying their dead. Wellington ordered his army to stand down, but kept everyone on the alert. Several times during the day there was a rush to arms when the French artillery started up, but each time it proved to be no more than harassing fire.

The day passed without event for the waiting troops, although back at headquarters there was a constant movement of senior staff officers and divisional commanders around Wellington's tent. As night came on and the soldiers settled down, thankful that they had survived another day within sight of the enemy, the lights burned late over the sketch maps and despatches as the Commander-in-Chief made his plans. He felt certain tomorrow would be the decisive day.

Again there was a morning mist and a stand to before dawn, but this time the growing light revealed a large scale movement of the French army to the south of their previous position. In that intuitive way he had, Wellington had anticipated this and had placed extra infantry and cavalry to the south of his own army.

Before long the cannonade began and with the usual drum rolls, bugles and shouts of "Vive, l'Empereur", a large force of French cavalry and foot soldiers crashed upon the British lines.

Crauford and his Light Division had been ordered to support in the south and Jack, Tom and the rest were soon sweating and straining at another forced march. A veteran beside Jack muttered, "I knew it, I knew it...always the same...bang go the French and in go the Light Bobs...always in the front where the work's to be done!"

On a flat, rock-strewn plain by the village of Poco Velho, the Division moved into squares. All around Portuguese infantry and the British 7th Division were being driven back. Only the cavalry under General Cotton had kept together and still constituted a challenge to the enemy. Crauford and Cotton, two hard but brilliant field commanders, found themselves virtually isolated. It was then Crauford had his finest hour with his beloved Light Division.

As the French charged in a mass, the British squares stood firm until they were within shouting distance of their enemy. Then those terrible, concentrated volleys rang out and the squares slowly retreated in perfect formation. They were set out in mobile echelons as though on a field day in England - so many squares firing, then retreating behind others who waited with loaded muskets to repeat the process.

When the French brought up artillery, the cavalry charged the guns and drove them back. The dark uniformed riflemen who had gained Jack's admiration when he first saw them in Portsmouth barracks, were skilfully used in small independent groups. They dodged and dived behind the rocky outcrops and picked off the French by hundreds.

The Horse Artillery galloped up and joined in the fray, dropping their guns into action and firing into the packed French troops from the gaps between the redcoat squares.

For two miles this brilliant and disciplined manoeuvre was carried out. Down in the squares the men worked like a well-oiled machine and cracked jokes or sang snatches of song as they fired, moved back, reloaded and fired again.

Jack saw at once the way disciplined troops could oppose a huge mass of badly led men. He looked around him at the faces of those who had joined with him from his Dorsetshire village. "What price for the old sheep folds now, boys!" he shouted. "You never thought six months back you'd be playing these games!"

A familiar face in Jack's column grinned back. "Ah! Jack lad, the sheep were a sight quieter than this lot. I think I'm stone deaf with all them guns a goin' off!"

Then Tom Eagan's sharp eyes spotted something. "Look now, to the right there; Sergint Hooper, there's something afoot in that great mob o' Frenchies!"

Hooper was up to the front quarter of the square in a second. "Hold your fire, hold it there, men! There's some of our lads in that lot!"

A two gun section of Major Bull's Horse Artillery had lingered for one more shot and the protective square of infantry had pulled back. The guns became completely surrounded by French cavalry when the young Captain Ramsay shrieked the order, "Cease firing, limber up, get 'em out of here!"

The infantry watched with amazement and then cheer after cheer rang out as the sweating gunners dropped their guns on to the limber hooks, leaped on their horses in the traces and, protected by their already mounted comrades, charged in a swirling mass of gun wheels, horses and flashing sabres.

They shot out of the tightly packed French like a shell from one of their own guns, Ramsay in the lead with his sabre going like a mad thing. Another piece of tradition was written into that day.

Back in the village of Fuentes, Wellington had more troops ready as his opponent, the redoubtable Marshal Masséna, made one last try for victory.

The Light Division had put paid to any success for the French on the southern front by the mauling they had given the enemy. In Fuentes itself Masséna fared no better, since the wild Irishmen of the Connaught Rangers, the fighting 88th and the Highlanders of the 74th Regiment plunged into the tightly packed streets and had a hand-to-hand battle royal until the entire village was once more in allied hands.

Wellington had been at every place where the fighting was thickest and had taken up his vantage point at Fuentes only 400 yards from the battle. The French tried a few more attacks with the remnants of Masséna's reserves, but by nightfall the end was in sight.

The prudent Wellington had his men work half the night to throw up earthworks and trench lines. His exhausted men stood to at dawn and watched the remains of the French army manoeuvring from side to side to find a way in. There was no gap left, no weak point in the firmly held line. By midday, in clouds of swirling dust, the French columns silently retreated out of sight.

Jack and the boys flopped to the ground and slept for several hours. Then they washed, ate, drank brandy, cleaned their muskets and talked endlessly of personal experiences and incidents in their first engagement, the battle of Fuentes de Onoro.

CHAPTER FIVE

Alarums and Excursions

Marching away from their first battle, the boys of the reinforcement draft felt they were now one with their regiment, the Light Division and Wellington's Army. They tramped along with the veterans of the 52nd, laughing and joking as though they had been campaigning for years.

Lord Wellington had hurried south with a few staff officers where a fresh battle was about to begin. He came to his southern army under General Beresford to advise, to watch over and if need be to take control of the battle. Albuera, as it became on regimental colours and war memorials, was another triumph for the British army although an even more costly one than Fuentes.

During the long summer days the northern army went into cantonments and spent its time on manoeuvres, sport and relaxation. In a bivouac area one night, just after the Fuentes battle, Sergeant Hooper called Tom Eagan across to a group of officers' tents.

"Now what would I have done wrong, d'ye think? Is he after makin' me a sargint or givin' me a flogging? He shared them chickens I got last night, so he can't complain about that."

The little Irishman strutted across to Hooper and looked up at the sergeant with a bland and disarming expression of innocence.

"Eagan, I seem to remember from your papers you were in service once," said Hooper.

"I was that, Sargint. A noble Englishman in me own Clonmel at home – fine fellow he was but a bit of a lad with the bottle. He used to clout us a bit when…"

Hooper cut short these reminiscences of Irish servant life and came to the point. "Captain Reilly, an Irishman like yourself, is without a servant right now; his own man caught a lump of shrapnel in the backside at that last party and is on his way to Lisbon face down on a bullock cart. Now I'll put in a recommendation for you if you'd like the job."

Tom thought around the situation for a moment, realised that a few extra luxuries might be to hand and weighed them against the additional work he would have to undertake. "There's just two things I'd like to know, Sargint. Can Molly come along as the officers' laundry woman and would I still be with me mates when the scrappin's on again?"

"Yes, of course, Tom. You're a soldier first, remember."

Hooper called softly into the tent and a tall, moustachioed captain strolled out. Hooper and Eagan saluted and the officer eyed the little Irishman for several seconds.

"This is the man, Sir," said Hooper. "Thomas Eagan. Came over on the draft with us and showed a good spirit at that last bit of a show with the French. He's been in service before, to an English gentleman in Ireland."

"Well I'm an Irish gentleman in Spain but I don't expect that'll make any difference," said Reilly. "He's not the cleanest looking of your bunch, Hooper, but no doubt he'll pass on a dark night. Does he drink?"

Tom cut in quickly. "Why, your honour, a drop hardly passes me lips. Just occasional like when this Spanish dust gets on me chest."

"Hold your tongue, Eagan!" barked Hooper. "I'll do the talking for you." He turned to the officer. "I wouldn't say he was the most sober of my little lot, Sir. But I'll keep an eye on that side of it for you."

"Right, he'll do. Have him report before dinner tonight. Any scrimshanking or larking about and I'll hand him over to you for a taste of the cat."

Captain Reilly turned on his heel and strolled back into his tent. Hooper led Eagan away and began to recite the list of duties for an officer's servant. A groom looked after the captain's horses, but Eagan was responsible for the baggage mule. At all bivouacs, except within sight of the enemy, he was to unpack the mule, put up the tent, make a clay fireplace, get wood and water, cook a meal, lay out dinner at night and wait at table. He was to clean his master's clothes and boots and pack everything neatly away each night in readiness for an instant move.

"God save us all, Sargint! Sure the work was hard enough back home where a dozen of us looked after the old master and everythin' to hand. I'll have no time for a bit of foragin' or scroungin', sure I won't."

Hooper laughed and slapped Eagan on the back. "You'll manage, Paddy or I'm no judge of men. Now there's one important thing I forgot to tell you. Captain Reilly has charge of a light comfort cart belonging to General Crauford himself. The General sets great store by this and has all his reserve rations, wine and such like on it. He won't have it with his own staff but insists on an officer being responsible for it. God help you if anything happens to one small item on that cart."

Tom joined his comrades and told them of what he called "me promotion!" He promised them samples of wine from the general's stock…"as soon as I've shaken down in the job, like."

The hot summer days rolled by and autumn was soon upon them. The men played football and the officers went horse racing or hunting. The officers of the 52nd were a modest crowd, but the gay young blades of the Rifles, like Captains Harry Smith and Johnny Kincaird, had packs of greyhounds, teams of fine hunters and were forever dashing off across the dry sierras after deer, hares or anything that ran at the sound of their hunting horns.

The French manoeuvred back and forth all down the line of the frontier between Spain and Portugal. Once, at Fuenteguinaldo, south of Ciudad Rodrigo, their artillery spotters called down a hail of shells on a bathing party that had found cool clear water in the shallow river. Nobody was hurt, but the sight of a crowd of half-pink, half-brown naked soldiers streaming back into camp brought cheer after cheer from the troops.

There were skirmishes and odd minor actions but never a major engagement.

Intelligence reached Wellington that the French had been reinforcing all through the summer. Because he had no new victories to signal back, a parsimonious government in England sent very few new men to the Peninsular. With his army stretched over a long front and winter coming on, the British commander was forced to act at all times with great caution. He tried to force the French into an attack on a number of occasions but they seemed unwilling to face the set piece battle at which he had become so skilful.

An attempt had been made that summer to take the great fortress at Badajoz but it had failed. In the north the other fortress of Ciudad Rodrigo was under siege, but spies and local partisans filtered into the British lines with stories of the size of the French armies – almost five to one against Wellington.

One evening, in the mid-September of 1811, Wellington made his decision; an orderly retreat back into Portugal, winter quarters and complete regrouping until he was ready to strike back and defeat his enemy on his own terms.

Fires were lit all along the line and the French watched these burning throughout the night. By morning their advance patrols were cautiously moving up among the smouldering remains of these fires, but the British were gone.

There was an attempt at pursuit, but the French marshals knew they could not feed their men, living on the land as they moved forward. So they also withdrew and the campaign ended with the cold winds coming down from the hills and the winter rains pouring down on the armies as they marched into towns and searched around for warm billets.

Up in the hills, the Light Division tramped back with the rest of the army. Tom Eagan complained bitterly to Jack and their comrades of the trials that had to be met by an officer's servant when every day brought driving rain and biting winds.

"Sure and I'd give a whole bottle of brandy for a bundle of dry firewood. We halts at nightfall an' off he goes. 'Get the fire goin', Eagan. I wants a shave an' hot water, Eagan. Cook me a fowl, Eagan.' Me blankets is wet too an' I've slept in 'em like that for a week. Ah! It's back to duty for me 'fore long. I'll take me hook wid me mates and the devil can look after Captain bloody Reilly."

Jack and the boys roared with laughter at Tom and his misfortunes. Every unit has a man who seems to attract a larger share of bad luck and yet somehow surmounts it. They are a cross between a scapegoat and regimental clown and unwittingly they are a great tonic to the spirit of the others. Thus was Tom as he trudged through the mud of a mountain pass, holding the headropes of his master's pack mule and the emaciated beast that drew General Crauford's light cart.

The column had slowed down to a walking pace as the tracks were narrow with precipitous drops on one side. At a bend in the track with a high rock wall on one side and a sheer drop on the other, the General's mule came to halt and decided this was as far as he was prepared to go. The pack mule ambled on so Tom let it go, concentrating all his energies on the stubborn cart mule. "Git on, git on, you long-eared heap o' Spanish leather. Git goin' there, yer foreign, stubborn, four-legged bastard!"

The column behind had ground to a halt and there were shouts of: "Clear the way there…What's afoot…? Who blocks the line?"

Jack and the boys broke ranks to lend a hand and there was much shoving and heaving of the immobile animal.

Captain Reilly and Sergeant Hooper strode up, the officer swearing as he faced his now frantic Irish servant. "Eagan, you Clonmel clown, get that mule on the go and careful with the General's cart. Do something, Hooper. Use your head, man. The whole division's perched on this track and we'll all be court-martialled if you don't get some action soon!"

Hooper took charge at once. "Belts off, men. Buckles outwards. Lay in to him now. Let him know you're master!"

Half a dozen soldiers began to lay about the mule with belts and musket slings. The animal shuddered a bit, snorted but refused to budge.

"I have it," cried Tom and, seizing a belt, he leapt on the mule with his legs dangling either side of the cart traces. Like a jockey at Donnybrook Fair, he drummed his heels into the animal's flanks and lashed about front and rear with the improvised riding whip.

The mule gave a snorting cry, arched its back, and jumped forward like a thoroughbred hunter. The troops scattered and cheered 'til the rocks echoed. But in seconds the mule had gone from stubborn immobility to a wildly plunging gallop.

Tom hung on to the mule's ears and the small cart swayed and crashed about him. The next bend in the track came up fast but the mule did not see it. With a wild leap Tom had flung himself to one side. The mule and cart went on.

There was a silence that seemed to last for seconds, then a dull crash somewhere far down in the rock-strewn valley. Tom picked himself up, rubbed his bruised head and put on his cap. The soldiers collapsed around each other in roars of laughter. But, looking black with anger and more than a little worried, Captain Reilly set off back down the track to report on the fate of one mule and one general's comfort cart to the general himself.

The column moved on and Tom caught up with his sole remaining charge, the captain's pack mule. An hour or so later a grinning Sergeant Hooper hurried along the line to tell Eagan his services were no longer required by Captain Reilly.

"The general's proper crusty about it, Eagan. Went for the captain like a wild cat. Captain wanted to have you flogged but the general wouldn't hear of it. Said if an officer was put in charge of something then he was responsible. Reckon you've come off well out of this."

Tom grinned all over his face and broke into a wild Irish ditty.

"You're a lucky devil, Tom," said Jack as he stepped out beside the now jubilant Irishman, "but from what I've seen of old Crauford he won't forget this in a hurry."

Neither did he, for, every time he saw poor Captain Reilly in the Light Division's line, he shook his fist at him and roared, "There he is, the rascal who lost my cart. I ought to have him court-martialled!"

The story is told that the unfortunate captain was wounded early in the next battle of the campaign. Seeing him carried off in a slung blanket held by four soldiers the general shouted: "Put that officer down. Get back to your duties, you men!" Turning to his ADC he continued, "That's the scoundrel who lost me my comforts cart!"

The army trudged on across the mountains and back down into the plains of Portugal. The rain turned to snow and the men marched with their blankets wrapped round them to aid the scant protection their threadbare uniforms gave.

As always on these retreats the food situation became a serious problem. There was a good deal of looting when they passed through a village and one night Tom joined his mess mates round the thin stew in the cook-pot with his entire cap filled with cayenne pepper. Before the others realised what he had acquired, he had tipped the lot into the stew with the remark: "This'll warm us all up—give a bit o' body to that tough lump of beef in there."

They ate their stew, for there was nothing else, but if Tom had not immediately produced a bottle of cold red wine to cool their burning mouths he would have taken some rough treatment from his angry comrades.

On another occasion a man came out of a small shed in a farmyard with a tale that it was piled high with freshly milled grain. Jack took a lantern and with two others went in to investigate. There it was, by the flickering light, a huge pile of what looked like wheat grain. They grabbed some empty sacks, ran forward and proceeded to fill the load. Then it seemed the heap was moving in a strange way; it seemed to be alive. With a shriek the first man dropped his sack and rushed through the shed door. He yelled only one word – "Fleas!"

In seconds Jack and the other two were flinging off their clothes and scratching like madmen. Some peasant women came out of the farmhouse and, to the delight of other troops, stripped the three men and plunged them into barrels of icy water. This, plus the vigorous shaking of their clothes, was a drastic but effective cure. The entire action was carried out accompanied by giggles from the women and roars of coarse laughter from the onlookers. The victims did not share in the amusement.

On another occasion a ravenous soldier made off with a beehive under each arm. The bees objected and he died in a matter of minutes from their savage revenge.

The Light Division took up their winter quarters in a small Portuguese town and a string of neighbouring villages. The quartermaster general moved ahead of the army to requisition the larger houses for the senior officers and his staff allocated the more humble homes for the rank and file. In the general scramble for a good billet it was usual for the quartering officer to indicate a whole street with a wave of his arm and leave the troops to sort themselves out.

Some houses had been left empty and locked, but a single shot from a musket opened most doors.

Jack, Tom, Molly and six other comrades made a rush for a soundly built two-storied house at the end of a street and hammered on the door. After a few moments the door was opened wide enough for Jack to wedge his musket in it and the frightened face of a middle aged woman peered out at them.

"No soldiers—no room, soldiers—my daughter very ill." The woman stood there hoping her few words of broken English had sunk in and she would be left unmolested.

There was something unconvincing about her manner and one of the soldiers at the back called, "Let's get inside, boys, I'm freezing to death out here. If we don't take this one we'll end up in a cowshed for the best billets'll be gone by now."

Jack firmly but gently prised open the door and they lumbered into the main living room. The owner fussed around and flapped her hands in protest. The troops moved through the house with experienced speed, noting the kitchen and the state of the cooking store, checking on the pump in the yard and laying claim to bedrooms.

Molly Eagan staggered upstairs with a huge bundle of personal stores and Tom followed, dragging a large leather trunk they had acquired somewhere along the line of march. Jack joined them in the large front bedroom where all three stood round a bed and looked down at a fully clothed young woman. The older woman bustled in and continued the protests about disturbing her sick daughter.

"She don't look very sick to me," said Molly. "Look at the bloom on them cheeks. She wants to come a marching with us, she'll know what bein' sick means."

Tom grinned wickedly at the group and motioned silence. The girl had turned on her side and with closed eyes was doing her best to look as ill as her mother claimed. With a shout Tom brought his hand down with a loud slap on the girl's ample rump and she shrieked as she leapt at least two feet in the air. Tom continued his cure by climbing onto the bed and tickling the girl until she was a helpless, wriggling, laughing mass of wildly disarranged clothes. The mother promptly fainted and was caught by Jack from falling to the floor.

"Sure it's a doctor I ought to be," cried Tom. "Isn't that the quickest cure you've ever seen?"

Molly Eagan's voice cut loudly across the laughter in the room. "That's enough of that, Tom! I'll be tying you down in the bed tonight, for I know you of old when a bit o' skirt's loose in a house."

The girl stood up and straightened her clothes, smiling with obvious coquetry at the group. The mother was restored in a few moments and resigned herself to the new lodgers. At least she felt reasonably safe for herself and her daughter with the strong-minded Molly under the same roof.

The unloading of a pile of rations and some looted bottles of wine went even further towards cementing good relations in the billet and, with rooms allocated and the fire roaring in the kitchen, a peaceful co-existence was soon worked out.

That night, while Tom snored heavily in the upstairs bedroom, Molly and Jack sat like old friends by the dying glow of the kitchen fire. They were finishing off a bottle of brandy, most of the contents of which had contributed to Tom's state of deep and undisturbed sleep. The other troops were scattered about the house, while the owner and her daughter had locked themselves in a single room at the front.

Molly was strangely quiet for once and Jack commented on this rare side of her nature.

"Ah, Jack, you think I'm a wild 'un all the time. You know me; a bit o' fun, a laugh and a drink. That's old Molly, they all say. But y' know Jack, I'm a woman too. It's when I gets in a house and sees furniture an' pots an' a kitchen stove all burning and warm like. It's then I thinks of home. Me an' Tom have been wandering an' larking around most of our lives. We've lived rough an' niver seem to have a roof over us for long. I had children once, but they all died. We was either in gaol or on the road. I don't think there'll be any more children somehow. There's been no signs for years an' it aren't for the want o' tryin' by that lively old cricket upstairs; drunk or sober, nobody could call my Tom lazy when he's abed."

She tipped the dregs of the brandy bottle into her tin mug and sat nursing it for a while and sniffing the fumes. "I'm gettin' old, I think, and likely a bit soft in the head. As Tom says, we'll have a lark or two and a drop to drink before this little caper is finished. But what about you, Jack? You're still a young man an' if you don't stop a bit o' French lead or go down with the ague you should be thinkin' of the future. Now I had a feelin' about that dancing girl of yours at Lisbon—what was her name, Rosa somethin'? She wasn't just a bit o' fun for one night, I said. I told Tom I reckoned you was tippin' your hat serious like in that direction. Am I right?"

Jack thrust a twig in the remains of the fire to get his pipe going again and stretched back in his chair to look at Molly. Her face was in profile from the light of a single candle and he thought that in her youth she must have been quite a beauty. For all her wild and often outrageous way of life, he had grown very fond of this fat, loveable Irish woman.

"Yes, Molly. You're right in a way. I only spent one night with her. Knew her for only a few hours; yet I often think about her, particularly during this quiet winter spell. I asked of all the new draft as they've come up from Lisbon but they say there's nobody of that name dancing in the bodegas. Reckon she's gone back to that village of hers and damned if I know where that is. Albergaria it was called, I wrote it down on paper to remember it in case we ever went that way. I'm told it lies somewhere to the north, near the coast."

"Why don't you ask the captain for a few days leave? I'll get a horse for you, see if I don't."

"It's no use Moll, we can't go more than five miles. Hooper told me that. No, it's a soldier I said I'd be and I'll take it all as it comes, same as you and Tom. We've a lot more to see yet and maybe I'll meet up with her again on the march. Come on Moll, me old love, let's to our beds. I can hear your Tom snoring from down here."

Molly got up and put her hands on Jack's shoulder. She pulled him down gently towards her and kissed him quietly and slowly. "God bless you, Jack," she whispered. "You deserve a good woman and I hope you gets your Rosa one day. I'll say a little prayer to Saint Patrick for you, or is it Saint Valentine? I niver was very good at me saints."

She went lumbering up the stairs as Jack blew out the candle and went to his own room. The old house creaked into silence.

The days and nights of winter went by with the troops of the Peninsular army thankful they were in houses and able to keep reasonably warm. In spite of bad weather, Wellington kept his commissariat on their toes and plenty of food came up through the long supply lines. Great stocks of ammunition were built up and months before the commander-in-chief had signalled for the siege train bearing guns that had laid by the harbour in Oporto for over a year.

It was when the troops saw these iron monsters on specially built carts with teams of up to twenty oxen pulling each unit that they realised the winter holiday was over. Over a thousand carts had been commandeered to move the guns and their mountings, powder and shot. They were moving in a northerly direction and the rumours spread like wildfire about where the next action would be. As always, the veterans were right for they had a way of interpreting the signs and movements within the army. Everything pointed to an assault on a garrison under siege and, as they left their winter quarters and marched over frosty roads, the name was on everybody's lips - Ciudad Rodrigo.

The campaign of 1812, a fateful year for Napoleon and his French revolutionary armies, began in the Peninsular within the first week of January. The British and Portuguese troops had left behind the comforts of the bedroom and happy hours round a fire as they marched towards the heavily fortified town with its great defensive walls and two flat-topped hills that lay to the north of the garrison.

Those two hills were heavily defended by French artillery and extensive earthenworks. Jack, Tom and the boys of the 52nd were formed up in a field and watched with mixed feelings as a number of Companies from the Light Division were moved off to help in the first assault on the hills during the night of the 8th of January.

Tom stamped his feet and banged his arms about as he cursed the cold night air. "By the saints, Jack, I'd sooner be off with the boys up them hills than standing about here freezin' to death."

The others agreed with him when the rumble and crash of shells, grenades, and guns firing in unison echoed down to the stationary troops. The night sky was lit by an increasing pattern of flashes and coloured lights. Sergeant Hooper was going the rounds with a rum jar and, as usual, prevented Eagan from filling two mugs at once in the semi-darkness.

"It might be a sight too warm up there," he said. "We've to stand here and keep a whole skin 'til they want us."

"Don't they want us, sergeant? Can we go home to bed?" asked a young lad.

"They want us all right, when they're good and ready. I hear it's trench digging for us when the boys get in sight of the town walls."

A veteran holding out his tin mug for a tot of rum spat contemptuously on the ground. "Trench diggin', that's sappers' work and Portuguese work an' suchlike. What's come to the men of the Light Division diggin' trenches when there's real scrappin' to be done?"

But trench digging it was, for days and nights under the heavy fire of the guns from the garrison walls. The earth was frozen and the surface hard to crack. They gradually worked deeper and dragged up sandbags, hurdles and sedge mats to consolidate the complex system of trenches.

Jack and his friends had seldom worked so hard in their lives. Often in the coldest hours before the dawn they slogged away with greatcoats and jackets off. Then they would dress completely, wrap a blanket round their shoulders and stand-to for twelve hours of daylight while an erratic rain of shells thumped and crashed around them.

They knew the next phase was in sight when the great siege guns opened up from their rear and started pounding away at the thick masonry walls to make breaches for the final assault.

Sir Thomas Picton's Third and General Crauford's Light Divisions were pulled out to the rear and rested for twelve hours. The 3rd was given the main breach and the Light the lesser breach to the left.

"Fix your flints, boys. Get moving." The order came down the line and again there was that nervous ribaldry from the soldiers. "Keep hold of me hand, Sargint, I'm 'fraid of the dark—Don't kill the women, boys, we're comin' in—" and from the irrepressible Eagan: "Me muskit's jammed, me powder's wet, I cannot fight tonight. Who's for a drop o' good French brandy at a guinea a swig?"

"Get along there, Eagan and cut the talk," shouted Hooper. "Keep together and heads down 'til we fire!"

The Third Division ran into a packet of trouble as they crossed two ditches with improvised planks. A hail of musket and howitzer fire crashed into them and they also found themselves surrounded by shells dug into the earth and fired by powder trains lit from the garrison walls. These exploded with frightening results and the whole mêlée was suddenly brought to a halt by a shattering explosion as a huge mine went off in front of the main breach. So great was the detonation that many of the French were killed at the same moment as their attackers.

The Light Division turned as the ground rocked and the night was made into day by this explosion. They watched with fascinated horror at bodies flung fifty feet and more into the air. On their front they had the easiest of the breaches for there were no ditches to negotiate, no secondary walls or minefields.

But a defended town is no country picnic and, as the 52nd came up to the flaming gap in the walls, they were met with a roar from point-blank-ranged cannon and the inevitable hail of musket balls. Down went the front ranks and then Hooper's voice was heard above the din. "The General's hit, make way there, boys; covering fire and fix your bayonets!"

Crauford had been wounded and Brigadier Vandeleur beside him. Jack whipped his rolled blanket from his knapsack and flung it down by the group bent over the commander of the Light Division. He was pushed on by the eager men behind and found himself running behind Tom into the gateways and streets of the town. If his blanket was used to carry off the general, then he felt he'd been of some help. There was no time now for thinking about anything except pressing forward as fast as possible and getting the frantic business over in the shortest space of time.

Other attacks from the south and east had also proved successful and where one moment all had been flashing fire and sudden death there was now a great rushing down streets, greeting of other regiments and the rounding up of nearly two thousand French defenders.

Jack was like an excited schoolboy, blackened with powder smoke and running with sweat despite the cold night air. He helped Sergeant Hooper get a column of French prisoners on the move back towards the breach and into the allied lines.

"Have you seen your mate, Eagan?" cried Hooper.

"I've lost him, sergeant. I think he's gone into the centre of town."

They both turned to the centre where all the sounds of a riot in progress could be heard. Muskets were being fired wildly into the air and flames were already lighting the scene from some of the unoccupied houses.

"I've to get the last of these prisoners back. Then I'll be looking in to see you boys don't get out of hand. If Eagan gets at the drink there'll be floggings by morning." Hooper marched briskly off and Jack joined a rush of cheering soldiers who were making for the main part of the town.

The butt ends of muskets had already dealt with the doors of the wine shops, and, from inside, the crashing of glass and the tossing of bottles from hand to hand meant the boys were in for a rare old night of it.

A small crowd of screaming nuns ran like scattered hens from a convent by the church, pursued by hatless and blackened satyrs with brandy bottles in each fist. Shops were broken into and their contents scattered in the street while men from a mixture of regiments argued and fought over their plunder.

Jack moved swiftly from scene to scene, feeling a little sorry for the inhabitants of the town, but knowing that a siege resisted meant, inevitably, the sack of a town and its attendant devastation.

He suddenly realised he had not eaten for hours and grabbed a large hunk of cheese as he passed an open shop. He was biting great mouthfuls from his cheese and thinking a bottle of wine would not come amiss to wash it down, when an unmistakable voice rose above the general noise of the streets. "Jack! Jack, me boyo! Up here lad, we've the best of everythin'!"

He turned around and looked the length of the street. A huge two-storied warehouse was halfway down and standing out from the line of houses. An upstairs doorway with a loading ledge and a beam with hoisting tackle jutted out in the centre of the building. It was from this that Tom Eagan swung like a tumbler in a circus. "Come on up, Jack!" he called. "All the boys is here and old Molly's in charge of the cook-pot. Come an' have a drink wid your ould mate, Tom!"

Jack found the entrance and climbed a broad-stepped ladder to the main loft of the warehouse. It was the most fantastic sight in the world, a veritable orgy of colour, sound and movement.

The great bales of cloth and boxes of stores had been hurriedly pushed to the walls leaving a large open space in the centre. Upwards of fifty soldiers, redcoated infantry, riflemen, a few horse-gunners in their high-waisted jackets, and Portuguese levies were scattered about the room. A dozen of the British soldiers' wives and camp followers had been joined by as many again of the more spirited local women.

The scene was lit by a number of flaring torches, a few lanterns and candles. The centrepiece was the height of folly itself; a great iron cauldron set on the wooden floor and a blazing fire beneath it made from the broken cases of wine bottles. Everywhere more boxes were being opened and clothing, furniture, trinkets, food and hundreds of bottles were changing hands. Some men had set up little booths like shops and held up perhaps a clock, a painting or a lady's dress with shouts of: "Who'll give me ten golden dollars for this fine thing?"

Several of the soldiers were wounded and lay amid the bales with the women making drunken attempts to bandage them and pour brandy down their throats to ease the pain. Tom swung into the room from his outside perch and leapt from bale to bale to greet his friend.

122

"Now isn't this a grand sight, Jack? Aren't we the lucky ones to find this place wid all these good things free for the askin'?"

Molly, resplendent in a tight-fitting dress from a high-born lady's house was alternately swigging from a bottle and tipping the contents into the giant cauldron of soup. She stirred the mixture which already contained flour, rice, vegetables and a good many litres of wine. The women around her were busy stripping chickens and skinning rabbits to throw them whole into the pot. A soldier discovered a large smoked ham hanging from the roof and hurled it neatly across into the pot, sending a great splash of the contents over Molly.

"You clumsy bastard!" she shrieked and hurled an empty bottle back at him.

A hogshead of fiery, half-matured brandy was broached by the simple method of firing a musket ball into it. Buckets were placed beneath the fountain and there was more than enough for everybody.

Jack sat down on a box with a beautiful glass flower vase full of wine by his side and both hands occupied with a haunch of ham. Like the rest of them he felt that this was fair reward for the fighting and risks taken an hour or so back.

One of the regimental drummers had found his way into the warehouse and with suitable priming from a bottle, began to tap out a lively rhythm. Somebody found a flute and one of the Spanish girls had a guitar. A wild, uncoordinated music competed with the general roar and dancing began. It was not the dancing of a salon or even a country jig at a harvest supper; it was a wild and uninhibited romp, making up for style by its noise and drink-inspired energy.

While some thumped and swayed around the centre of the room, others moved bales of cloth to construct little love nests, and couples disappeared into the shadows for more private pastimes. A girl with all her upper clothing hanging about her waist ran shrieking across the room pursued by a redcoat minus his trousers. At the same time Tom Eagan was executing a particularly complicated dance movement of his own invention on the top of a pile of boxes. It was at that moment the party came to an abrupt end.

The fire under the cooking pot had been steadily consuming the floorboards and main beam underneath. In the extra smoke and general heat of the room it had gone unnoticed. With a crash like the mine that went off at the main breach walls, the entire floor split, sagged and went crashing down to ground level in a shower of sparks, bundles, boxes and the tumbling figures of the revellers.

Jack felt the floor moving as the first crack came and leapt instinctively to some high stacked bales. As these slid into the abyss he rode down with them and, apart from a crack on the head, was unhurt. Screams, shouts and groans rose out of the debris and Jack set about tearing aside timber with his bare hands. One of the first things he found was a pair of fat legs that waggled frantically. He seized the feet and heaved with all his strength to extricate a wildly cursing Molly who emerged wearing only a shift, the beautiful Spanish dress having stayed down in the rubble.

Tom emerged with a bleeding head neatly framed in the shattered remains of the girl's guitar. Others crawled and heaved themselves out to stagger into the street.

The saying that the Devil looks after drunken men was proved that night, for, miraculously, nobody was badly hurt. The large amount of liquid in the stew-pot put out the worst of the fire and a few buckets of water did the rest.

There were a few broken bones and the wounded soldiers were in a worse shape than before. The latter were dragged out into the street to be laid on piles of wool from the split bales and left to beg assistance from the few stretcher bearers who were still sober enough to go about their duty.

Jack rounded up his friends who were now laughing and joking about the whole affair. "Look at ould Molly," called Tom. "Isn't she the grandest sight there? Like one of them girls in a painting wid her clothes all gone!"

Molly shrieked as she realised her ragged shift was insufficient clothing for such a place, then she dashed across the street and through the smashed door of an empty house. She soon emerged dressed in a long white night-gown and a fine Spanish officer's cloak with gold fastenings.

"There now, an' I'm dacent again. Let's off to another party where I can show off me fine new clothes!"

They all moved down towards the town centre where a great deal of noise indicated there was plenty going on. As they came to the main square, Tom held up his hand and stopped them in their tracks. "I smell trouble," he said. "There's provost troops in there. I think we'll find a quieter billet."

The centre of the square was a heaving mass of soldiers shouting, swearing and some firing muskets into the air. But a large force of provost troops and sergeants from reserve regiments were rounding up men with a steady efficiency. In the middle of the riot General Sir Thomas Picton himself, and Colonels Barnard and Cameron, were mounted on their horses and laying about them to right and left with broken lengths of musket barrels. This salutary treatment plus Picton's famous bull-like voice were restoring order from what had nearly become a dangerous situation.

Jack, Tom, Molly and a handful of their closest friends crept silently down a side street. They soon ended up squatting in the dark on the floor of an empty house and passing a brandy bottle from hand to hand. Except for an occasional giggle or a belch, they were silent and remained unnoticed.

The rioting and looting had been stopped before they reached the serious stages of a mutiny. Those unlucky enough to be caught would obviously feel the lash on their backs before the next day was through. But at dawn, with the inhabitants tidying up, the troops drifted in small groups back to their lines.

Junior officers and sergeants attempted rudimentary roll calls and got their Companies into a rough and ready order. Wellington himself rode out to the corner of a cross-road and watched with fascinated horror as the cream of his army marched by.

Their uniforms, threadbare before they had started the assault, were now in rags. All were filthy dirty and most were without caps. Yet every man had a musket or rifle, even though many a fixed bayonet bore a ham, a whole cheese or half a young pig. A few carried little bundles of loot—perhaps a bird cage, a clock or badly damaged painting. Bottles protruded from jacket pockets everywhere and two enthusiasts were prevented from rolling a large barrel any further just before they came level with their commander-in-chief.

Some, whose uniforms had disappeared altogether during the night, were dressed as priests, Spanish noblemen and even in the full-length dresses of the city's grandest ladies.

Wellington turned to his aide and remarked, "I am a commander of the scum of the earth, enlisted for drink."

The Light Division formed up in their bivouac area and were then told the sad and sobering news that their tough old commander, Thomas Crauford, had died during the night from his wounds received at the approaches to the breach. The 52nd's brigade commander, Vandeleur, was to recover from his injuries, but the loss of Crauford was felt strongly from Wellington himself down to the youngest drummer in the Light Division

A quiet and serious body of troops packed its equipment and loaded their wagons for yet another long march in the Peninsular War.

CHAPTER SIX

"Reunion"

The army had not been on the southward march for many days when small drafts were pulled out of each regiment to act as escort details for additional guns and ammunition of the siege train. Jack was among this party and said farewell to his comrades as he tramped off the line of march. Sergeant Hooper was the only one he knew from their Company, most of the draft being made up of new men sent in to fill the gaps in the Companies after Ciudad Rodrigo. They headed west in the cold stinging rains of the end of winter. An unknown colonel of ordnance and two junior officers led the contingent of just under 200 men.

After a week of marching, the cold winds had a tang of the sea about them and they knew the coast was not far away. The first group of heavy ox-drawn guns and ammunition carts had already been met and sent south with a small escort of redcoats. Bivouacked that night in a tiny, poverty-stricken village, Hooper and Jack went in search of some wine to make their meagre rations more palatable. They had come to the end of the village, and a cross-roads, and were about to turn back, thus abandoning their quest, when Jack saw the signpost. One name was unknown to him but the right fork was clearly marked with a name that had been in Jack's mind for weeks - *Albergaria*.

He tugged Hooper's arm. "Hey, sergeant! Look at that. Albergaria. That's the place. That's where she lives. Albergaria, plain as I can read."

Puzzled, Hooper looked up at the signpost in the fading light. "What the Devil are you on about, Wheeler? It's just another cross-roads by a dirty little village in this dirty, Godforsaken country. What the hell's with you, man?"

"That's where my woman lives. Rosa. Rosa Silvero. We met at Lisbon the night we landed. This is a great thing, sergeant; for I never thought I'd get so near."

"Well this is as near as you are getting, my lad. I'll not have you tramping off into the night after a bit of Portuguese rump. Come on, Wheeler; this a'nt like you. Thought you was one of the steadiest in my lot. Come on, wheel about and let's get back to billets 'fore we lose our way in this blasted country."

Again Jack grabbed the sergeant's arm. "But sergeant, we'll not move 'til morning. There's twelve hours yet and I'd go like the devil to get there and back. Let me off the hook just for a night. I swear I'll be back before daybreak."

Hooper jerked his arm away with impatience. "Now see here, Wheeler. Enough of this from you. If it was Eagan or one of the other drunken fools I'd expect this sort of thing and clamp 'em down hard. Now I've always trusted you for the good soldier you've become. I shouldn't tell you this, but I've your name down for corporal with the Company officer. Don't disgrace me for some local bitch and spoil your chances with the regiment. Turn about to billets, man, and forget this mad scheme."

They did not exchange another word as they walked back down the village street and into the barn where their party was settling down for the night.

Jack slumped down on his pile of kit in a corner and munched hard tack biscuit by the light of a guttering candle. He was trembling with excitement and anger, determined not to turn away from this remarkable stroke of luck. Hooper had settled down with a small group round an upturned cask and the rattle of a dice could be heard. Quietly and very naturally Jack got up and slowly walked to the barn door. He turned and noticed the sergeant was bent low over the dice and about to throw. In a second the heavy door was opened just wide enough to slip through. He was soon hurrying through the darkness of the village.

A guard lantern swung from the mayor's house in the centre of the village where the officers were billeted. Jack kept close to the opposite wall and was almost past the house when there was a clatter of feet and the guttural sounds of a corporal changing the guard. A voice rang out, "Halt, who goes?" The corporal and a private of the guard came striding across the street, the former swinging a small hand lantern. He held up the light and peered into Jack's face. "Now where would you be off to on a cold night like this?"

"I'm looking for the officers' house," said Jack.

"The officers' house; well ain't that nice? Goin' to join 'em for dinner, was you? Ah! 52nd are ye? You'll be one of Hooper's lot. I should put you in the clink for the night, so I should. But I'm a gentle soul at 'eart, ain't I, soldier? Now get back to your billet or you'll be up for a taste of the cat by morning."

Jack decided on one last desperate throw. "I've a message for the officer commanding the escort draft. I'm to give it to him personally."

"Oh! Is that the way it is, mate?" said the corporal. "Just you tell it to me and I'll pass it on through the sergeant of the guard."

"I'm to give it personally," said Jack.

The corporal, a slow thinker at the best of times, stood clutching his lantern and shifting from one foot to the other. "What do you make of it, soldier?" he asked the guard detail.

There was no reply, for the infantryman had seized the opportunity to slip a few paces back into the shadows and was leaning against a wall in a deep sleep.

The corporal wheeled about and roared into the night air. "Soldier! Wake up, blast you! I'll have ye flogged! I'll have ye on guard for the rest of this trip!"

"Just dozed off, corporal," whined the soldier. "I'm mortal tired an' done two guards this week a'ready." The corporal cut short this common grouse of all soldiers. "Damme! You'll get my boot at your backside if you do that again! Get back to your post an' look sharp about it!"

As the soldier marched off with a clatter of arms and boots ringing on the cobbles, a door opened in the big house across the street. Framed in the yellow candlelight was the short, plump figure of the colonel of the escort draft. He had a large glass of wine in his hand and was smoking a cigar. "What goes on out there?" he shouted. "Is that the guard? Who the devil's making all that noise?"

"The devil have his guts, an' yours too," whispered the corporal. "Now you've roused him, the worrying fool. Come on, at the double." Jack and the corporal moved towards the steps and the latter addressed the officer in his best regimental manner.

"Corporal of the guard here, Sir. On me rounds, Sir. Found this 'ere rascal wandering round your billet, Sir. Says he has a message for you."

The colonel peered down at them. "Hold your lantern higher, corporal. What d'you mean, message for me? How can he have a message for me at this time of night? My two junior officers are here with me. There isn't another officer for miles around. How can he have a message? He's not a runner, is he?"

"No sir, he ain't no runner. One of the draft, Sir. 52nd with Sarn't Hooper's lot."

"Bring him up here, man," said the colonel with a note of petulance creeping into his voice.

They climbed the steps as the colonel drained his glass of wine. Jack was sweating in spite of the cold night, but determined to have his say.

"Let him speak," said the colonel.

"Stand up straight," barked the corporal. "Colonel give you permission to speak! Give your name and regiment—say your piece and keep it short!"

Jack cleared his throat and went straight into his appeal. "Sir. Private Jack Wheeler, 52nd Regiment, Light Division. Ask permission for one night's leave from duty, Sir. We're hard by the village of Albergaria and I've a friend there, Sir. A very close friend. I could maybe borrow a horse and…"

The Colonel cut him short. "Albergaria. Yes, I know it. It's a fair ride from here. I didn't know we had any troops there. Is your friend on the siege gun lines?"

Jack's mind was in a whirl. He could see this hundred to one chance slipping by. "My friend's not a soldier, Sir. It's a woman. She's my woman. I thought, perhaps…"

"A woman!" roared the Colonel. "Blast my eyes! What is this bloody army coming to? You have the audacity to ask me for leave to go chasing one of your sluts of women? I'll have you in irons…"

"I'd be back before daybreak, Sir. I could…"

"Hold your tongue! Don't interrupt an officer!" shouted the corporal.

The colonel spluttered and waved his empty glass in anger. "I've a good mind to put you in the guard room for your insolence. I come out here for a breath of fresh air. You kick up a racket and disturb my billet. Take him away, corporal. March him back to his lines and tell his sergeant if I hear any more of this nonsense, I'll have the cat out of its bag before we march tomorrow. Be off with you!"

The colonel gave a final snort and turned to go through the door of his billet. It was then Jack acted in desperation and made a fatal move. He took a step forward and grabbed the colonel by his sword belt. A wine glass crashed to the ground and the now infuriated officer spun on his heels. The corporal leapt forward and gripped Jack by his jacket collar, frantically looking for somewhere to put his lantern and release his other hand. At the same moment he bellowed, "Guard! Turn out the guard! At the double, guard!"

Jack was now the centre of a confused, shouting mêlée; the colonel backing into the doorway, the guard blundering up the steps from the temporary cellar guardroom with the duty sergeant in full cry at their head. Jack was seized on all sides and with feet scarcely touching the ground was bundled into the guardroom and manacled to an old iron bedstead.

He had taken to many aspects of a soldier's life with enthusiasm and after nearly a year in the Peninsular was a long way from the callow country yokel of Dorset who had joined up; he had always avoided "the clink".

Tom had talked of experiences in almost every gaol in Ireland and not a few in England; tales of incredible squalor and harsh living. But Tom was at home in such a setting and upon release was always refreshed and ready for more wild behaviour.

The idea of being tied up, even for one night, seemed a terrible thing to Jack. He dozed fitfully until the rattle of arms brought the night guard to the dismissal parade and the duty sergeant came in to unlock the handcuffs. The sergeant, a tall, angular Scot with red hair and a straggling moustache, made no comment as he released Jack. He handed the prisoner a piece of dry bread and a tin mug of nearly cold tea.

"What will it be, sergeant?" asked Jack. "What d'ye think will happen?"

"You'll be charged," was the only reply.

"What would they charge me with; deserting a post? I was not for duty last night."

"Worse 'n that soldier. Ye struck an officer. They tak' right bad at strikin' an officer."

"Will I get the cat?"

"Ay! Mebbe you will. Or you might be hung."

Jack was speechless for a moment. Confused and appalled at the speed of events over the last few hours, he had terrible visions of the next hour passing with the same pace and relentless fatalism. A few words of a charge, some barked orders and a rope thrown over the branch of a tree—then the chair kicked away and him dangling and fighting for life.

Nearly a year of campaigning with hardly a scratch; appalling conditions and not a day's illness—then a swift end like this, an end of disgrace and ignominy.

He sat for some time with his mind a complete blank, oblivious of the clatter and shouting in the street outside the guardroom cellar. He made no resistance when the duty sergeant, a corporal and two privates came in, pinioned his arms and marched him out into the dawn light. At first he did not even react to the sight of over one hundred men formed up in three sides of a square, the single drum on the pavement and the junior officers standing together by the steps of the mayor's house. Then he saw "the three maidens", the triangular flogging frame and he felt a great wave of relief that he was not to be hanged.

Jack was placed in the centre of the square with an armed sentry stood on either side and a corporal immediately behind. He caught sight of Sergeant Hooper who eyed him with a face black with anger. The parade was silent as they waited for the colonel to open the proceedings and, after a few minutes, Hooper came to attention, marched across to the two junior officers and saluted. There followed a brief conversation and the senior Lieutenant nodded and led the sergeant into the house. Ten minutes went by, broken only by an occasional cough and the clink of arms. Once a voice on the right flank muttered something about "...be little 'nough time for our breakfast with this bloody nonsense," to be cut short by a roar for silence from the duty sergeant.

The colonel, the lieutenant and Sergeant Hooper came down the steps, Hooper marching smartly on to his place. Everybody came to attention and the colonel said, "Let's get this business over. Duty sergeant, read the charge."

The duty sergeant, with much stamping of feet, moved forward to face Jack and his escort. He did not reveal that reading was the least of his talents, but held a piece of paper at arms' length and spoke most of the routine words from memory and long practice.

"Sir! Charge under the acts of war and army discipline...serving of His Majesty, King George...Private Jack Wheeler...52nd Regiment of Foot...did strike his superior officer...insulting manner...etc."

The colonel walked slowly across the square and stood a half dozen paces in front of the prisoner. "Have you anything to say, Wheeler?"

Jack swallowed hard. "Very sorry, Sir. Would like to apologise to you, Sir."

The Colonel turned slowly on his heels and looked at the assembly of men. He peered at the closely lined ranks, nervously swishing the air with a short riding whip. Then he turned to Jack and said, "Your sergeant spoke highly of you. Asked me to be lenient. I will be lenient, but you must learn—" he paused, raised his voice for the benefit of the assembly, "—and you men must learn, particularly you newcomers to the field; you must learn that your officers are here to look after you. They think for you. Plan for you. They take responsibility for everything. But they are your superiors and must never be approached, except through the proper system—through a sergeant, who will bring you to your officer in a proper manner. As for touching an officer—that is striking an officer and it is a serious crime in the army."

The colonel was a simple man at heart. Most of his life had been spent with moving stores and signing papers. He had never held an active command of troops in battle and he was both nervous of this side of authority and yet clearly enjoying his moment of absolute power.

He waited to let his words echo round the expressionless faces before coming to the final part of his address. "I said I would be lenient with you. We march in less than an hour, so look sharp everybody. A hundred lashes, sergeant!"

"Sir!" roared the duty sergeant.

Jack was hustled quickly to the triangular frame, coat and shirt removed and leather thongs tied to his wrists and ankles. As the two drummer boys each removed a short cat-o-nine tales from a black bag a corporal slipped a musket ball into Jack's trembling mouth. "Chew on that, lad. Makes it easier."

A third drummer began a regular rat-tat-tat as the sergeant turned smartly for the order to begin.

The colonel walked slowly across and looked for some time at the figure stretched on the frame. His lips went tight and there was a strange look on his face, half anger and half compassion. Then to the entire parade's amazement he shouted, "This man has a clean skin. Never let it be said I was the first to break it. Take him down and mark him for guard duty every night of this trip!"

The colonel strode quickly across the street, up the steps and disappeared into the officers' house.

Commands rang out and the troops doubled back to their billets for a hurried breakfast and to pack for the march.

A sweating and nervously excited Jack Wheeler was released from the frame and had his clothes flung at him by an impatient corporal.

"I thought Eagan was a lucky devil," said Hooper as they hurried down the street. "The old man must have liked the looks of you. In all my service I never seen the likes of that; why I've known men get 400 for less than you did."

It was not until Jack was hastily stuffing himself with fried pork and packing his knapsack that he too realised how close had been his escape from the harsh punishment of the times. Hardened old soldiers had survived dozens of such floggings, but to many a young man the first taste of the cat not only marked their bodies but had a brutalising effect on their minds. It was a quiet and thoughtful soldier who fell in with the column and marched down the village street to salute the colonel on his horse by the steps of the mayor's house.

As they came to the cross-roads with the signpost that had prompted the events of the night, it was almost with relief that Jack saw the column swing to the left. After what had happened, he felt the chance of marching through Albergaria and maybe doing no more than waving to his Rosa would have been unbearable. He felt it better to remain in ignorance of whether she was there or not.

Just over a week later, having escorted a long line of bullock carts laden with ammunition, Sergeant Hooper brought his small party to the dismiss in the square of the small town of Elvas.

The scene was a familiar one to all but the new reinforcements; troops everywhere, commissariat stores set up in barns and farm buildings, staff officers hurrying to and fro on their horses and whole regiments moving about in apparent chaos. Another action was in the wind.

Hooper told the escort party to draw any kit they needed, stock up with fresh rations and have a few hours free in the town before reporting to the headquarters of the 52nd at the eastern end of the main street.

Jack took a number of newly-joined men under his wing and led them through the packed streets of soldiers and baggage wagons.

He boasted of his experiences and the knowledge of his way round an army in cantonment.

"Here's the ration stores, my lads. If they're giving any extras, go for the biscuit. It lasts out better than the salt beef and you don't get so thirsty."

He led them into a large barn where two quartermaster sergeants checked their names at the door. The long dark building had trestle tables set out and men were queuing for their hard tack and a few litres of wine. An argument was going on by the wine barrels where a six foot Irish rifleman was brandishing the largest goatskin seen in the Peninsular and demanding that when filled it was his normal ration. The little storeman was giving as much as he got and Jack hurried forward when he recognised the voice of the man whom some mistaken authority had thought fit to put in charge of the wine.

"Hey! Tom there! Tom! Have you a spare goatskin and a drop of blackstrap for an old comrade?"

Tom looked up and shouted back with great glee. "Jack, me boyo! So it's back to the regiment is it and good to see you. I heard tell it was a flogging you had on that escort job. We're all fine and kicking here. Plenty of grog an' a good little temporary job for me, in me proper place a' guarding the army's precious wine an' keeping these thieving rogues from gettin' too much, what they wouldn't appreciate anyways."

The lanky rifleman shook his empty goatskin at Tom and demanded his due. "You little Clonmel runt. Would you cheat a Dublin man of his drop of rotten wine? I'll have you stuck backside out o' one o' them barrels if you don't fill me skin."

Tom grabbed the skin and placed the opening under the tap of the nearest barrel. He had to tip the cask, so that much of the rifleman's ration was only dregs. As he worked away, he kept up a babble of commentary for his old side mate. "Did ye iver see the likes o' this? A lanky great rifleman wid a wineskin bigger'n old Molly's belly and holdin' half the regiment's rations. Sure he can wash in wine, cook his beef in it, bath in it an' still get drunk for the rest of this week. Here, gi' me your cork an' on your bloody way; I've real soldiers to look after!"

Jack moved round to the row of wine barrels and asked for news of their own group of friends. "There's nothin' much afoot," said Tom. "It was all marchin' here and marchin' there, 'til we got to this place. Molly's in the town sellin' a few bits an' pieces we got on the way. Sergeant Kelly's wife had a child on the march, 'bout fifty miles back. A fine little fella she had an' weaned on blackstrap, I reckon."

"What's the news of the battle, Tom? I hear it's not far from here if it comes to a fight."

Tom poured himself and Jack a tin mug each of wine and ignored the patient soldiers in the queue. "The old 'uns was right, Jack. It's Badajoz. That bloody great fortress and the city beyond. Old Nosey's had a couple of goes at it before. The officers say their noble Spanish friends calls it 'Proud Badajoz'. I did a spell in them trenches down there, Jack. Right stinking, muddy hole it is, wid fog and mists all over and Frenchies bangin' shells down on us. No, I reckon it'll be a right old bash around with plenty o' widders, even if we ever get inside the place. Bloody Badajoz, I calls it."

Tom had settled down on an upturned cask, lit his pipe and smiled blandly up at his friend. Oblivious of where he was, this was the sort of happy state he enjoyed most of all. A friend for an audience, a full stomach, a roof over his head and ample drink to hand. He was oblivious of the long, shuffling queue of soldiers who had come for their wine ration until an angry quartermaster sergeant strode up and kicked the small wine cask from under the little Irishman.

"Get out o' here, you lazy, drunken Irish tinker. I give you a job to do and there's a line of men stretched halfway to the general's house, waiting for a drop o' wine."

Tom picked himself up. "Why y'r honour, I was just passin' the time o' day wid an old comrade o' mine that has come down wid them big cannons an' glad to be back among his own folk, as I was just a' sayin'…"

"Out of it," roared the quartermaster, "you've a tongue like a Portuguese fisherwoman. Here you, there, front rank man. Take over the job and look smart about it."

He strode away leaving a delighted private of the 51st in charge of the wine barrels. Tom slipped three filled goatskins from under a pile of sacks and led Jack away through the crowd into the open street.

"Now there's a thing, Jack. Shortest job I've ever had for I've not been there above an hour. Ah! Well, I feel like a stroll round this town. Let's go find old Moll an' see if she's any money left on her."

They made their way to the 52nd's lines where Jack reported back for duty. He flung his kit beside Tom's in an overcrowded cottage billet and they set off towards the centre of the town.

A scream of laughter from the semi-darkness of a cook shop gave the two men the location of fat Molly. They swaggered in to where she was holding court to a mixed bag of British Dragoons, German Infantry and Portuguese Artillery. She dropped the half-eaten pigeon pie that she had been wielding with both hands and gave a shriek of welcome. "Ah! Isn't that me own darlin' Jack back wid us. Me own special love for which I'd soon be leavin' that skinny little brandy-pickled cock sparrow, if I didn't have a soft spot for him too. Gintlemen! This is me husband and this our special friend Jack, as what joined along of us in ould England and 'as stuck fast wid us ever since."

Tom, ever loquacious on his own but frequently silent when his wife was spouting forth, grunted a greeting and managed to get his hands on the half-eaten pie from under his wife's nose. Jack sat down beside Molly and she greeted him with one of her bear-like embraces. The allied soldiers looked on with much amusement at this strange trio.

Molly ordered wine all round and some hot, spiced pork. She asked Jack about his trip as escort to the guns and heard the story of his attempt to visit Albergaria. When he told of his narrow escape from a flogging, she cut in with, "Tom's had a taste o' the cat while you was away. 'T was the funniest thing I ever saw."

"Funny Moll? You found it funny to see Tom flogged?"

"No love. That weren't funny. They beat 'im 'til his back was raw an' I gave that provost sergeant a bit o' my mind. No, it was the reason for him gettin' the cat we all found such a joke."

The mixed group of soldiers stood up and made their farewells, realising that Molly was no longer there to amuse them but obviously wanted to attend on her husband and friend.

She waved gaily to them and turned back to tell Jack of yet another of Tom's extraordinary adventures. "Y' see Jack, it were like this. We was halfway down from that Rodrigo place an' fair worn out wid marchin' and precious little food about. Tom was out foragin' in a wood early one evening and found a plump billy goat which, o' course, he grabbed and made off wid. Course, how could he know it belonged to ould General Picton, y' know, Sir Thomas of the Third. Tom was on the edge of the wood, by a little stream, an' draggin' the goat along by its beard an' the goat kickin' up the seven sounds of hell when the general rides up with his officers. He shouts to Tom, 'You there, put down that goat you thievin' varmint!' Course Tom feels safe on t'other side o' the stream an' it's gettin' dark so he shouts back, 'Gawd bless your honour, I'll gladly share it wid ye and send a leg for your sarvint to dress for your dinner if the bloody animal will just stand still a minute!'

"Well, the general and the officers start shoutin' and screamin' at that an' Tom get a tighter grip on the goat's beard. Then the goat gets tough wid Tom an' drags him along the ground an' into the stream where they thrashes around like a couple of wrestling men at Donnybrook fair.

"If Tom had let go 't would have been all right but he hangs on to the devil in horns and the officers send a troop of Provost 'cross the stream an' the general gets his goat and Tom gets a floggin'!"

The object of this story looked up from his empty plate, drained his glass and said, "You've done enough blatherin' to last the night through, Moll. I'm fed an' I'm fit an' glad to see me mate Jack wid us again. Let's go round the taverns and have a bit o' fun."

They moved off into the crowded part of the town, Jack greeting old friends and feeling like a man who has come back to his family after a long absence. In the milling crowd around the square, they heard the noise of singing and guitar music above the general din. It was not yet dark and they could see a good deal of activity where one of the side roads joined the square. The trio made an instinctive movement towards the music and found a large, open-sided cart wedged in the narrow street, with a Portuguese guitarist, a flute player and a drummer perched on barrels at one end. The dance rhythm of the Volera struck a chord of memory in Jack and he elbowed his way through the crowd of wine-swilling, cheering redcoats.

There she was, as he remembered her that night in Lisbon nearly a year ago- dark hair, pale white face and those brilliant, flashing eyes. He struggled like a madman to get near the edge of the cart, pushing soldiers to right and left and getting involved in a series of minor scuffles. "Rosa!" he shouted, "Hey, there Rosa! It's Jack. Down here, Rosa!"

He had succeeded in getting a few feet from the cart when the dance reached its climax of swirling skirts, frantic music and the roaring from the spectators. She had not noticed him and after bowing to the audience who threw showers of coins on to the platform, she took a towel from the guitarist, wiped her sweat-soaked face and moved to the rear.

A tall, sharp featured sergeant in the Portuguese cavalry held up his arms to catch her as she jumped from the cart. He flung a bright red cavalry cloak round her shoulders and they began to elbow their way through the crowd to a smart open air restaurant on the edge of the square.

Jack heaved his way through and stood by her table, just as she and her companion had sat down.

"Rosa, do you remember me, Jack—in Lisbon? By God, it's good to see you again."

She looked up at once, puzzled for a moment then smiled slowly and blushed a deep red. She held out both her hands and Jack grasped them as she spoke. "Oh! Jack! Si! Si! My English soldier." She went into a torrent of Portuguese, then reverted back to her broken English. "A long time. You not killed in battles, in fighting? You not hurt in fighting? I am happy to see you now. I think—to see you again—not possible—the soldiers go from Lisbon—now so few— I ask many and show your badge—they say much fighting for you—many killed—I pray you not dead— Oh! Jack, I think you go to fighting again soon— everybody say at Badajoz, across the border— Spain…"

Her gabbled, excited words were cut short by the Portuguese sergeant, whose first puzzled and then angry expressions showed he clearly disapproved of the revival of old love affairs. He cut in with some sharp questions in their native tongue and was promptly told it was none of his concern.

Jack took a chair and sat at their table; his feelings mixed by the delight at seeing the girl again and the fear that her relationship with the cavalry sergeant was of a permanent nature. "Rosa. This sergeant...is he...I mean, would you be his wife?"

She flung back her head and laughed with those pealing notes that had captivated him at their first meeting. "No! I not married to any man. Why I get married? What good for me get married when war and fighting in my country? This sergeant come from village near my home—you know, I tell you once—Albergaria—he look after me. So few soldiers in Lisbon now; Bodega where I dance, all closed—I come on, what you call it, baggage train, with Portugal soldiers to Elvas here—two, three days. He just a friend—look after me—Why you worried if I married?"

Jack looked embarrassed, but was determined to keep a grip on the situation. He meant to find out how things stood and make his own plans. He put his next question with candour, for he felt that if they were to link up again after even the brief interlude of last spring, he should know exactly how things were with the girl.

"You in love with this sergeant, Rosa? You ever sleep in bed with him?"

She held his hand and smiled gently at him. "No,

Jack. I think he like to sleep by me, but no—not this man."

"Perhaps others?" he asked.

Her eyes flashed with a sudden anger he had not seen in her before. She broke into fast, imperfect English, the phrases pouring out in sharp little bursts—"Yes, I sleep with other soldiers and Portugal men. Why not? You not my husband. You not even— what you call—in French, fiancé—promised in marriage—you love me one night, only one night. I love you then but you go away—your regiment you say, must go to be soldier—course I sleep some men. You ever been on baggage train—cold nights— everybody sleep together—sometimes I make love with man—not often—but sometimes."

She took his hand again and her voice grew quieter. "I never make love like when you come my room, Jack. I never have all the night with a man like when you come to me at Lisbon. That night, Jack, you marry to me—like man and wife. Yes?"

The Portuguese sergeant had been vainly trying to get the attention of a waiter and at the same time was straining to follow the conversation between Rosa and the English soldier. His English was very limited, but it was obvious even to his dull wits that there had been a close, if brief relationship between the two and it looked ripe for revival. He got up sharply and kicked his chair back. He glowered across to Jack and spoke in thick accents. "You—Inglesi soldier—go— go 'way—Rosa no want you—Inglesi pig—go or I kill you!"

Jack also leapt to his feet. This was simple enough; he had seen the situation before and he knew what the outcome would be. Soldiers frequently fought

147

over the momentary favours of their women, usually when the bottles were empty. But here it was a genuine desire on his own part to be rid of this inconvenient second suitor. The table went over with a crash. Rosa slipped skilfully to the shelter of the doorway and the two men met headlong.

Jack tried the conventional approach of bare-fisted fighting he had learned with the shepherd boys on the Dorset hills. A couple of sharp crunches to the sergeant's jaw sent the man lurching backwards to return with a blazing fury. Hats flew off and they were at the close quarters the Portuguese needed as being more in line with his style of combat.

They looked for a moment like wrestlers, straining swaying until the local man had a lock on Jack that threw him in a swinging arc to crash into a pile of flimsy chairs. It was going to be no holds barred for the sergeant came running in with feet flying and aiming a large cavalry boot at Jack's head. A momentary turn, a lightning movement and Jack caught the force of the boot on his shoulder and not the head it was intended for.

As the momentum carried the sergeant forward, Jack seized the other flashing boot and twisted hard, bringing the man crashing down beside him. They rolled around the restaurant forecourt, punching and heaving, getting to their swaying feet only to crash down again.

Already a cheering crowd had formed, with Tom and Molly elbowing their way to the front. Molly gave a yell as she recognised the dancer standing in the doorway. "Lookit now, Tom! Over there! That's what he's fightin' over—his Lisbon woman, Rosa. Isn't he the grandest fella to fight a great rascal like that for his girl? I'll lay you'd not put up your fists for me now, would you?"

"Get on wid you," shouted back Tom, "he's doin' fine. But watch it boys, for that's a Portuguese he's fightin' an' there's quite a few of 'em around; so stand by for fireworks!"

The "fireworks" as Tom put it came in a few seconds when the Portuguese sergeant, having just had a chair smashed over his head, slipped a hand to the back of his belt and produced an ugly, broad-bladed knife. The crowd shouted the one word "Knife!" Then came a hush as the sergeant crouched in the stance of a skilled knife fighter against the unarmed Jack.

They circled for several seconds until the sergeant thought he saw the opening he was waiting for. As he leapt the Englishman dived low and the knife came down on the already bruised shoulder. The thick epaulet on Jack's coat saved him from a serious wound, but he felt the blade slip through the thick material and a sharp pain as it made contact. He drove a terrific blow at his opponent's stomach and felt the man crumble. In a flash he joined his fists together in a tight hand clasp and brought them down with all his strength on the lowered head. The sergeant sank down like a pole-axed ox.

At the sight of the knife the now large circle of redcoats had moved instinctively forward, ready to come to the rescue if needed. A number of Portuguese troops had also closed in to take the part of their own champion.

The collapse of the Portuguese sergeant became a signal for the battle to open and in seconds all hell was loose. Tables and chairs, bottles and crockery flew like musket balls in an engagement with the French. Tom plunged into the uproar and dealt several smart cracks with a broken chair leg at a writhing group of Portuguese. Then he got to the dazed and bleeding Jack and dragged him through the crowd and into the side street at the back of the flat-topped cart.

Molly came running up and rendered first aid using the quick and simple expedient of tearing a large piece from her petticoat, smashing the neck from a bottle of white wine and bathing Jack's battered face. "Gi' me a hand wid his coat, Moll," cried Tom. "It's that shoulder I want to get a look at."

They sat Jack down under the cart and eased off his red coat. The wound in his shoulder bled copiously, but it was not a deep cut. There was more tearing of petticoats from Molly with the remark, "It's stark naked you'll be havin' me in a minute Jack, if I goes on at this rate."

"Quit your blatherin', woman and get his poor ould shoulder mopped up a bit," cried Tom.

Molly was splashing cold wine all over Jack, but her knowledge gained over the past year of dealing with wounded soldiers proved a rough but effective treatment. She bandaged the shoulder with strips of linen while Tom administered brandy from the inevitable bottle he was always able to produce "— for times of trouble and distress."

"We'll have to get some horse liniment at them terrible bruises he's got," said Molly.

"Ay, I know the very fellow that'll have some. The captain's groom has a good stock of such things."

Jack was murmuring his thanks and returning to a more normal state as they heaved him to his feet and set off for camp. Suddenly he stopped and cried.

"Rosa. I must get back to her. We can't leave her in the middle of that fight. The Portuguese may get her. I must go back!"

"You're coming wid me, Jacko lad. Molly'll go for Rosa. Come on, you great cow, you've been in worse fights than that. I'll set off down this street with old Jacko here an' you go back and bring his pretty lady for him. Sure won't that be the finest cure for our gallant boyo!"

Molly grinned and was thrusting her way back into the fight in a few seconds. She grabbed Rosa who was still cowering in the doorway. The Portuguese sergeant was nowhere to be seen, though it was feared he had not risen from where he had been struck down and there was now a heap of struggling, swearing soldiers on the spot.

As the girl was dragged by the Irishwoman into the side street, the cry went up, "Provost, boys. The guards are here. Beat it up now!"

A half-Company of provost troops had been rushed from the camp and waded into the battle, dealing out blows with cudgels and arresting innocent and guilty on sight.

Before the fight had been stopped, Rosa had linked up with Jack and Tom. She stopped for a moment in front of the still dazed soldier and held his bruised face in her hands. He smiled down at her and she softly bent towards him and kissed his mouth.

The rather touching little scene was broken by Tom shouting, "That's enough love play for today—anyways, there's plenty o' time for that at night. Let's be gettin' on our way a bit quick like 'fore them blasted provost varmints get their dirty hands on us."

The quartet hurried off through the town to their cottage billet on the outskirts. Tom and Molly gave up their room to Jack and after treatment of his wounds he was made comfortable in the big double bed. With a clean shirt on his back and glass of rum inside him, he sat up like a wounded warrior, thoroughly pleased with himself.

Molly cooked food and Rosa waited on him. While the rest of the soldiers in the billet were in the town, the four of them had a pleasant evening with glass and pipe. Molly, for all her crude ways, was an excellent seamstress and soon had Jack's torn coat neatly stitched up.

Around midnight the Irish couple crept quietly away to sleep on heaps of straw in an empty stable.

Jack, drowsy with wine, lay on his pillows holding the girl's hand and not saying a word. The candle stuck in a wine bottle sputtered out and Rosa stood up for a few moments. Even through his half-sleeping state, Jack sensed the same feeling of excitement he had known in that tiny room in Lisbon when the only sound was the swish of the girl's clothes.

She slipped into the large double bed and Jack felt her long hair on his face. The instinctive tight embrace brought a sharp, hot pain to his injured shoulder that caused him to cry out.

"Oh, Jacko!" she murmured, "Poor Jacko. You still have pain. I will be your nurse. Make you better soon, better for me."

"I'll be all right Rosa. Right as a fiddle with you around. But why do you call me Jacko?"

She laughed quietly. "Tom call you Jacko. I call you Jacko. Always. I call you Jacko."

"Always, Rosa? Will you stay with us now? Move with us, like Molly. She'll look after you when I'm away. You're a strong girl and it's not a bad life. Will you stay for me, Rosa?"

She was quiet for a long time. Then she whispered, "I stay, Jacko. I always now your soldier's woman. One day, when war finish, we get married. Now I stay with you."

With his uninjured arm he held her very close in and in minutes they were asleep.

CHAPTER SEVEN

Proud Badajoz

Jack Wheeler awoke at dawn with a wild hangover, a sore face and a shoulder that seemed to be on fire. Apart from these aches and pains he felt as happy as on any day since he took the King's shilling.

His beloved Rosa was singing quietly as she moved about the tiny cottage bedroom, putting his kit together and making tidy what was to her the first home she would have with her English soldier.

The door was kicked open and Molly waddled in with a jug of hot coffee and a plate of fried bacon. Tom followed on her heels, fully dressed for parade but in place of his musket he was clutching the inevitable bottle of brandy.

"Now, Jacko, me lad! How's the old body this cold spring mornin'?"

"The fitter for seeing you and Molly and ready for a bite of breakfast."

The Irishman took a swig from his bottle, wiped the top with the cuff of his coat and passed the brandy to Jack. "Here, have a lick o' that, for you'll be needin' it. An' get that breakfast over sharp for we march agin' in the hour. There's a few floggin's goin' on in the town; some of the lads what was foolish enough to get caught by them provost bastards in the fight last night. Now seein' as we had nothin' to do with that business, we must get you on parade and lookin' fit like a soldier."

"Is the whole regiment moving, Tom?" asked Jack.

"The whole bloody army's on the move. Baggage an' all. Molly'll take Rosa along of her. The trenches by Badajoz is near finished and we're makin' camp outside the city. So out o' that bed an' let's get you dressed."

Tom and the two women hustled around and got the protesting Jack to his feet. They dressed him and Molly cut up a sheepskin to put under his coat where the straps of his knapsack came over the injured shoulder. His musket was retrieved from under the bed and the two men joined their comrades in the street.

Tom gave a playful slap to Rosa as he passed. "Don't worry a bit, Rosa, me beauty. Tom'll look after him an' Molly'll take care o' you. We're off to work like jolly soldiers all an' we wants a drop of hot food ready by nightfall."

Rosa ran out to Jack and kissed him passionately in full view of the crowd of soldiers pouring out of billets. A cheer rang out and there were bawdy cries of "—lookit now to Wheeler, the lucky devil's got himself a real beauty—I'll trade my wife for that one, Wheeler—now who'd a' thought our Jack would get a fine piece of bed meat like that?"

The voice of Sergeant Hooper could be heard from the top of the street and the whole party clumped off to their duty, with the women standing in doorways as though their menfolk were weavers off to the mill or miners to the pit.

Fortunately for Jack, the march was not long, and the next three days spent on putting the finishing touches to the trenches around Badajoz were arduous but not as telling on him as a battle would have been. The mists rolled up from the Guadiana river and concealed much of the dirty, waterlogged work from the eyes of the French gunners. When the mists lifted, it rained in long, steady downpours.

As they splashed around with their spades, often up to their thighs in stinking water, the grumbling infantrymen were fortified by an almost endless procession of rum jars. Tom worked like a beaver to do his own and often Jack's share of the work.

On the third day, Sergeant Hooper took pity on the groggy-looking Jack and sent him back with messages to the baggage train where the main camp lay on the higher ground at the rear.

The drying of his clothing by a fire and the ministrations of Rosa brought him back to a state of fitness at least as good as any of his comrades.

Then there was a lull of twenty-four hours while Wellington put the final touches to his plan and rested his picked divisions for what he knew was going to be one of the roughest fights of the campaign. The outlying defences of the city had been taken by storm, the heavy guns had battered the necessary breaches in the outer walls. Now those breaches could only be taken by direct attack; by men running forward and forcing their way through a defensive system that had been skilfully built up over many months. As a dandified young officer remarked to his companion while they rode back to camp, "It's going to be some party!"

On the morning of the 6th April, 1812, the order went down the lines. "It's tonight!"

There were very few last minute preparations to be made, so the men sauntered about the camp as though on exercise in England. The few who could write sat scribbling pathetic little letters that would take weeks to reach their homes and would, in too many cases, be the last message their families would receive.

Regimental bands played light airs evocative of a more green and peaceful country and a curious, quiet sadness came over the large camp of waiting men.

Jack sat under the baggage wagon with a sad-faced Rosa in his arms. He consoled her in the semi-jocular way that most of the men with wives or women were doing; pointing out that however rough the battle went, they were bound to come through unscathed. However, he had given to her safekeeping his small store of money with the thought that she would not starve if he failed to return.

A few men played cards and one or two small parties were fortifying themselves against the night's work by lively drinking sessions.

Molly found her Tom in the centre of one of these bottle-happy groups and dragged him away to the wagon lines. "Come an' make love to your old wife, Molly," she said, "for who knows if I'll ever see you agin' wid this terrible fightin' to be done?"

The inevitable coarse remarks that greeted this invitation had no effect on Tom, who suddenly got up, put an arm around his wife's ample shoulders and shouted back to his friends. "Ye can keep the rest o' that bottle I bought ye, for you're a drunken lot o' rascals an' I'm off to spend an hour wid this beauty of a wife I've had these many years."

The pair of them made a homely picture as they strolled off into a quiet part of the baggage lines at the edge of a cork tree wood.

Working parties were already moving off at dusk, but the planned assault time was postponed from seven thirty to nine. Final and often tearful farewells were said when the troops were ordered to remove and stack their knapsacks in the rear area. Then, without drums or colours, the men of four divisions and some Portuguese detachments moved off in silent columns into the mist-shrouded night.

The Third and Fifth Divisions had been given tasks on the far side of the fortress, but the job of getting into the main breaches had been ordered to the Fourth and the invincible Light Division.

Scaling ladders were collected from a great pile at the approaches to the corridor that led to the deep and wide ditch before the breaches. Jack and Tom seized one of these and before it was swung onto their shoulders, they briefly shook hands. There was no time for courtesies and these would have been out of place with two such close friends; just a "Good luck, Tom" and a "You too, Jacko, me boy", and they slipped and slithered towards the waterlogged ditch.

Like the beginning of some great ceremonial display, a single explosion from a gun started the grim night's work. A huge star shell lit up the closely packed ranks of men and then a concerted crash of artillery and exploding powder barrels rang across the entire front. Hell followed.

The leading files went down by the dozen and those behind hurled ladders across the ditch to get in close and cut the slaughter to the minimum. But the defenders worked as frantically as their attackers and poured canister and grapeshot into the struggling mass. Tightly-packed lines of French infantry manned the walls, each with eight loaded muskets enabling them to keep up a rapid fire. In no time the great ditch was a smoking grave for the mounting piles of dead and badly wounded men.

Jack and Tom had been blown half out of the ditch by the first explosion but regained their feet by hanging on to their ladder. Tom had a cut over his left eye and Jack was desperately sucking in the night air where he had been knocked breathless. They flung down their ladder again and held it in position like a bridge while a dozen men scrambled across. Shouts and cries, groans and muffled screams were almost drowned by the noise from the guns of Badajoz. Above all this the bugles continued to sound the advance.

Small groups of men, some with their officers, some on their own, had miraculously come unscathed to the very entrance of the breaches. It was they who saw by the flashing lights of the enemy guns that their task had only just begun.

The French had worked hard since nightfall and the gaps in the walls had been sewn with hundreds of sword blades fastened to thick planks of wood. More planks were lashed around the walls from base to summit and thickly studded with long nails, farm harrows and every piece of sharp metal in the town.

As the now maddened troops tried to rush these curtains of death, the well placed guns inside the town cut swathes through the attackers like a reaping machine.

Tom felt a burning pain in his head as he received the second wound in a few minutes. He staggered back and Jack caught him. By the light of a flare he dragged his Irish friend behind a pile of dead redcoats and ripped a shirt from the nearest corpse. "Here, Tom lad. Lay still and I'll stop the bleeding. It's only a couple of cuts as far as I can see. Let me get this dressing on you and you can get to the rear."

Tom lay still for a moment in the shock state of the wounds, but in a few seconds he was groping for his musket. "I'll not go back now we've got this far. An Irishman never deserts a fight, by God! I've a drop o' rum in me canteen. Hand it up and we'll get back into the scrap!"

They each took a swig of rum, got to their feet and rushed forward yet again. This confused dashing to and fro seemed to go on for ever. The murderous fire from the walls never slackened and the British casualties kept pace.

Once Tom and Jack became separated. Their scaling ladder had been smashed by a shell and Tom blown down into the ditch to disappear under a pile of bodies. Jack blundered across to a group of 4th Division men, reloading their muskets as they crouched under a pile of debris.

"Here's one o' the Light bobs!" cried a corporal. "How goes it on your side?"

Jack slipped down beside them and set about priming his own musket. He shouted back above the noise of the battle. "I've been in a few scraps since I stepped ashore, but, by God, this is a dirty one! I've lost me mate I've had for over a year, I've lost me Company—I think we'll all be cold meat by morning!"

A bugle to their left sounded for yet another charge on that terrible night and scarcely thirty unwounded men from a variety of regiments made a concerted rush for one of the open breaches, leaping over dead and dying figures by the flickering light of enemy guns.

In seconds a third of their number had fallen and the remainder dropped to their knees, levelled their muskets and fired through the breach at point-blank range. Their target was a French cannon whose crew were in the act of reloading.

The French gunners fell to a man and the corporal leading their party gave a loud, "Hurrah! Follow me boys—in with your bayonets!"

He rushed through the narrow gap, followed by a dozen or more men, now maddened to a point where all reason had gone. Jack had lost his bayonet and was in the act of wrenching one from a dead soldier's musket when a mine exploded at the entrance to the breach. A great flash, a chorus of yells and yet another small attack had come to nothing.

The explosion blew Jack and two others into a rolling, struggling heap—one with his coattails on fire. All three scrambled to their feet, beating out the smouldering coat of the man who laughed hysterically. In the confusion he did not think to throw off his jacket, but leapt about like a madman. A musket ball whistled and the man's laughter stopped short as he fell forward with a neat round hole in his forehead.

Jack was aching all over, parched with thirst and blackened by powder smoke. He suddenly felt lonely and very afraid in the middle of this confused, death-ridden assault. Regiments like the 52nd and the Light Division itself had always worked best and felt that supreme confidence that comes to well led troops when they attack as one body. Familiar faces around gave a sense of security in the roughest fight. But amid the chaos at the foot of these high stone walls, where communications were reduced to the odd shout or bugle call, it was only individual bravery and a sort of frightening madness that kept these small groups in the attack.

Jack crawled under a partly smashed cart, took a long drink from his water canteen, then carefully primed and loaded his musket. This drill-like action settled his jumping nerves and he peered out into the smoke and flashes to get his bearings. He thought for a long time of the possibility of lying there in comparative safety until the fury of the battle died down. But it seemed as though the assault was going on for ever—until all were killed or the castle blown up. Ciudad Rodrigo had had its moments of terror, of swift and bloody death; but they had fought as a regiment and charged shoulder to shoulder to carry the fortress there in a series of swift blows.

Drenched with sweat and still shaking from the shock of what he had come through, Jack suddenly decided he was not going to be killed. He felt that curious sensation of so many soldiers in the heat of battle who see dozens die around them yet cannot believe that it will happen to them.

He crawled out from his temporary shelter and ran with a crowd of ghostly figures towards the original breach where he and Tom had lost their ladder. Against a background of blazing powder barrels which lit the scene like Dante's Inferno, he found Tom, scarcely recognisable under a coating of his own and other men's blood, thick mud and powder black.

"Arrah! Tom, old lad! Are you still alive?"

"Is that you, Jack? By Jasus, I've been in some scraps before, but this takes all hell!"

Jack recognised Sergeant Hooper, black and besmirched as everyone else with a broken arm held in a musket sling and a rag bandage for a hat. "What Ho! Wheeler! Still on your feet? There's one of our officers hard by here getting a crowd of lads together to have one more go at this breach. Look lively boys and fix your flints!"

As they shuffled along to join a party of barely two score of men, of which over half were wounded, Tom and Jack briefly exchanged words to tell how they had survived so far. Tom had been buried in the great ditch for half an hour and had nearly suffocated in his struggles to get to the top of the parapet.

They formed up and Hooper checked that every man had a musket and bayonet. The young officer waved his sword and back they charged, firing from the shoulder and thrusting their way into the smoking oven of the breach. As they gained the entrance and leapt for the piles of rubble they were greeted with the same murderous fire from tightly packed French infantry and an artillery piece firing grapeshot from the ruins of a blown up house.

Down they went like ninepins, Jack feeling a dull thump in his left side just below the belt. He fired his musket at the shadowy mass of French troops just visible inside the breach, then he heeled over with the rest.

Tom was beside him in a flash and roared hoarsely at his friend. "So it's my turn to act nursemaid now, Jack! Where did the bastards hit ye? Here, give me your hand and I'll have you out of this."

Jack groaned and lay like a dead weight and it was all Tom could do to get him laid out on some planks. By the light of a burning piece of wood he located the ugly gash in his friend's side. He poured raw spirit, his universal cure for all ills, over the wound and shouted close to Jack's ear, "'Tis but a scratch, Jacko. The ball has passed by ye and gone out at the back o' your coat. Heave up on your elbows, lad and I'll have a bandage round to stop the bleedin'!"

Back in the quarries at the approaches to the assault lines, a grim faced Wellington checked midnight by his watch.

Staff officers had galloped back and forth with reports of the ever increasing casualties. By a rough count a third of the Light Division had fallen. The commander-in-chief gathered a group of senior officers around him. "It's no good," he said, "I should never have sent men into that place. Sound the withdrawal."

Liaison officers rode back to the inferno and soon the bugles were calling back the tired men.

Once there was a lull in the hail of shot from the walls around the main breaches, the astonished troops thought they heard a British bugle sound in the town itself. Officers and men stopped in their tracks, looked at each other and strained their ears as it sounded again. Then a flurry of mounted officers came riding in from the far side of the fortress with the fantastic news that the Third and Fifth Divisions had broken through and were swarming into the town.

They too had gone through a terrible and costly experience to gain the castle and the town. But the defences there had been lighter than the massed

French troops at the main breaches. The stubborn refusal to give in at the frontal attack had enabled these other assaults to succeed.

In the Light Division, surviving officers rallied the remnants of their Companies and went back once more to the main breaches, only to find them empty and unguarded. A cheering and hysterical mob, many of them lightly wounded, swept like a torrent past the wrecked guns and dead soldiers, in through the castle, and on to the now crowded streets of the town.

What followed has often been regarded as one of the blackest incidents in the history of the British Army. But who can judge what state of mind men are in having fought as they did with such intensive fury against an unresisting defence for over two hours.

Badajoz had always been hostile to the Allied armies and the French Governor, Phillipon, had ordered his troops to resist to the end. This lack of surrender until overwhelmed left the city open to sack by the ancient rules of war.

Thirsty, blackened troops made a thorough job of it.

Whilst Tom had been giving rudimentary first aid to his friend, the withdrawal had begun. They stumbled to their feet, made their way back towards the quarries to be met by the rush of troops returning to the breaches. They joined in to find themselves in the thick of the main body, that lurched into the town and deployed like streams of lava into the many side streets.

The chaos of the battle was replaced by a new sort of chaos. Down went the doors of the drink shops and taverns. Out came the casks of every kind of drink, to be broached on the spot by a musket ball and to flow until the very gutters ran and men splashed happily around.

Fires broke out and looting began on a scale that had never been seen before. The many shops in the centre of the city had boarded up their fronts and barred their doors. This had no effect on the plundering hordes who smashed in every obstacle and the merchants' goods were in the streets in minutes.

A few came downstairs and opened their shops, thinking in some curious way that there was trade to be done. No sooner were they behind their counters than they received a musket ball at point-blank range or were skewered on a bayonet and tossed with their goods into the street. Soldiers took over shops themselves and played at shopkeepers until their drink-crazed comrades tired of the game and dealt with their own kind as they had the original owners.

Even before dawn lit the terrible scene, the riot had taken a firm hold and become a mutiny when groups of officers, attempting to restore order, were fired upon by their own troops.

Hundreds of screaming women were prised out of hiding holes, raped and passed onto the next crowd of drunken troops. High-born ladies fought in their rooms with fire tongs, their husband's swords, or anything that came to hand while the furniture crashed around their ears.

The more serious looters, some of whom were joined by their women from the camp, kept clear of the drink and set about the business of filling handcarts with portable valuables. Money chests, gold plate, church ornaments, rich tapestries and valuable paintings were spirited out of the city in a steady stream to be hidden in the baggage wagons of Wellington's army.

Jack and Tom had careered around with the main mob for a few hours, slaking their thirst with any drink that came to hand. Tom was intrigued with it all - the size and appalling ferocity of the debauch.

"Now this is the wildest thing I ever did see, Jacko!"

"Wild is right, Tom. I won't say the folk here haven't deserved a right drubbing. But some of the lads are getting out of hand and it's all a bit ugly for me. I mean, cracking away at the Frenchies is one thing, but these are civilians, ordinary people."

They paused in their tracks as a large window opened in an imposing house. Hoarse shouts and screams were heard from the upstairs room. Then Jack and Tom had to leap to one side as an entire four-poster bed came hurtling to the ground. Shouts of laughter from above and the splintering of wood at their feet were capped by a woman's screams from within the wreckage of the bed itself.

The mattresses and bedding had broken her fall and the terrified wife of a Spanish grandee emerged from the debris and, clad only in a night-dress, ran up the street and into the night.

Tom found this very funny and cackled with laughter. "That's a rare sight, to be sure. She'll not get far in that rig."

Jack leaned against the wall, feeling desperately tired and his wound was beginning to ache. "I'm all in, Tom lad. Let's get a few dollars together and get back to our women. This business has been a bit rough for me."

Tom heaved his friend upright and they staggered into one of the quieter streets.

Tom was torn between leaving what promised to be the wildest riot of even his wide experience and the loyalty of standing by a friend. In truth, the double wound in his head was throbbing steadily, so he grabbed a large sack from the gutter and set off in search of loot.

"Keep by me, Jacko boy. We'll just have a bit of a scout around for what's to be had and I'll get you back to your Portuguese beauty. She and Molly'll get us on our feet again."

They rummaged around a number of small shops but troops had already swept through this part of the town and taken their pick. Just as Jack, now sick with fatigue, was ready to drop in his tracks, the experienced eyes of Tom noticed some loose floorboards in a jeweller's shop. A thrust with a bayonet and the boards were soon up and stacked under the shop counter. "Find a candle, Jack. I think we're in luck," cried Tom.

Jack stumbled about the shop and rummaged in drawers. He found a candle stump, lit it with a fusée match and they peered into the hole in the floor.

Tom's swift, searching hands produced a brace of fine silver candlesticks, some mixed cutlery in rolls of silk and a small leather bound box. "This is it," said Tom. "'Tis heavy enough for what I think it is."

A jab with the bayonet had the lock free and the yellow candlelight showed the equally yellow gleam of tightly packed gold coins.

Tom straightened up and broke into a kind of jig. "Hurrah for ould Ireland and God bless all poor soldiers on a night like this!"

Jack staggered to his feet and, although feeling near to collapse, joined in his friend's pleasure.

"That's a good little reward for a hard night's work, Tom. Let's sling it in the sack and we'll be away before some drunken bastard has it away from us."

With dawn breaking, the two weary, battered looters staggered through the streets until they came to a now wide open main gate at the side of the castle. Officers had organised stretcher parties from supply troops, engineers, and those men who had not joined in the mad rush into the town.

The pair picked their way through the melancholy business of sorting dead from wounded. Nobody paid any attention to them as, although obviously wounded, they were able to make their way by their own efforts.

The sky was streaked blood red with the early sun on light clouds, as though a reflection of the colour and fury of the night's events. Smoke rolled above the city from where a muffled roar could be heard, punctuated with odd explosions and the crackle of musket fire.

At the main camp the plump Molly and slim-built Rosa broke away from a group of anxious, tearful women to rush forward and hurl themselves at the two battered figures.

Jack was on the point of collapse when Rosa reached him. She held him up in her strong arms and frantically kissed his dirt-stained face.

Molly gave one of her bear hugs to little Tom and, practical woman that she was, greeted him with, "So I'm not a widder after all. I hope you've a present for old Molly in that bag o' yours."

Tom grinned through a face as black as a chimney sweep and gave his woman one of his hefty slaps on her rump. "Ay! Molly, we've got a neat little haul all right. But we're both near killed with that fight an' ready to die right here. Gi' a hand wid old Jacko now, for he's a worse state nor me."

Molly swung round to where Rosa was trying to keep her man from sinking to the ground. "Bring him here, Rosa. Put him up on my back. I've carried this little runt home many a time when he's been too drunk to walk, so I reckon I can manage Jack on a pick-a-back."

Rosa and Tom heaved the now unconscious Jack onto the Irishwoman's broad back and they set off for the baggage lines.

The handful of surgeons and medical orderlies were working on the badly wounded at the breaches, so Molly and Rosa set to with pans of boiling water and torn rags to clean and bind their own menfolk's injuries.

Within the hour they had swallowed a few mouthfuls of food, some sips of brandy and the two warriors were in a deep sleep under the shade of the baggage cart.

By the second day the city was a ruin. Still drunken soldiers were being hurled from top floor windows by their own comrades or quietly murdered in cellars and hovels by the vengeful survivors of the garrison.

A horrified Wellington was told the full story and sent in a large provost detachment. A gallows was erected in the main square and, after a number of swift hangings, the now utterly exhausted and satiated troops made their way back to their own lines.

Chapter Eight

High Summer and Deep Winter

It took almost two months for the army committed at Badajoz to recover from the action. While Wellington manoeuvred his other troops to maintain the split in the main French forces occupying Spain, his veterans of the assault recovered from their wounds, ate well and enjoyed the now warmer days that heralded the Spanish summer.

When the drums and bugles roused them to the march again the troops were already showing a healthy tan. In tattered uniforms they set off once more on a northern route across the rivers of eastern Spain towards the city of Salamanca.

Rosa's presence with the army was accepted in the 52nd Foot as were the many other liaisons that had come about between local women and the British redcoats. Although not on the official strength of their regiments, these supernumeraries were regarded as extra hands for cooking, laundering and the host of general duties that kept the baggage trains moving and the troops happy.

The terrible casualties of Badajoz had made widows of a number of the official wives, but within days of that battle they had all remarried. Mrs Estler, wife of a sergeant killed at the first assault, proudly announced that Corporal O'Brien had become her fifth husband of the campaign. Stories were told of a comely woman in the 95th who had recently married her tenth soldier... "And all British!"

High summer and days of scorching heat saw the dusty roads of Spain again covered by long columns of marching men. Many tramped along stripped to the waist, laughing, singing and shouting bawdy remarks to the women on their donkeys or riding atop the great ox-drawn baggage carts.

As night approached the bugles rang down the columns for the halt. In the cool of the evening men put on their shirts and jackets, piled arms and set to with their womenfolk to fetch water, make fires and lay out their single blanket on a pile of dried ferns.

All would be a-bustle as cook-pots were set, a stolen hare or partridge flung in to join the occasional pork or, more often, tough beef in the communal stew. Hidden bottles of liquor were unearthed and the small groups settled down to drink, play cards, gossip, occasionally fight or, more often, clown about until the night sentries were posted and those not for duty could roll in their blanket and sleep under the brilliant stars.

The married men and those with unofficial attachments would sometimes bother to put up tents or make little gypsy style encampments around the wagons.

Rosa took quite naturally to this hard but healthy life. Jack fussed around her and frequently went out of his way to acquire some extra delicacy from an officer's servant or get the wily Tom to ferret out such luxuries as cheese or fresh fruit from sources known only to himself.

The Portuguese girl was popular with the Company and while the men lay around smoking and the practical Molly patched uniforms, she would get her guitar to play and sing to them.

Jack would sit back with a proud, often smug expression when his beauty had the centre of a group of tough soldiers. He kept a close eye on her on such occasions for she was not amiss to directing her song at one particular man and start those tricks of coquetry that had so fascinated him at their first meeting. But it had been made abundantly clear that she was "Wheeler's woman" and any tipping of hats in her direction would be met with a fury that would stop little short of murder.

Tom Eagan passed the days happily, marching and singing, his nights spent on short spells of poaching, looting and his usual immoderate drinking. As they swung along one day Jack remarked that his friend had kept clear of trouble with the authorities for quite a while.

That same evening an incident occurred which reassured everybody that there were few dull moments in this campaign when Eagan was around.

The army had speeded up its rate of advance and the ration wagons, cutting across country from the coast of Portugal, were not always linking up on time. This had happened again and as men fell out for their meal, they knew it would mainly consist of biscuit and the leather-tough salt beef kept for emergencies.

Then the order came down to slaughter a limited number of the oxen and the cook-pots were going in double quick time.

Sergeant Hooper called for a man, a butcher in civilian life, who normally carried out this task. He was not to be found and the irrepressible Tom jumped forward. "I'll fix the ould cow for ye, Sargint! Sure there's hundreds o' such beasts I've killed before on me master's farm in Clonmel. A muskit ball in the right place, a good sharp knife and three willin' lads to lend a hand an' I'll have you feastin' like the Duke himself!"

A weary and bone-riddled animal was released from the shafts and Tom put on a leather apron with much dancing and fooling around until he had a large audience. The animal eyed its murderer with an indifferent expression until the Irishman swung his musket up for the death shot. At that moment the ox stamped the ground and lowered its head, just as the musket went off. The ball whistled across the camp and brought men running from other regiments. The ox charged forward, bringing Tom down and half a dozen standing around him. It then plunged off, knocking over piled arms, cooking pots and officers' tents, in a wild dash back and forth in the whole Company area.

"Eagan!" roared Hooper; "I thought you knew how to handle beasts! Get up, man, and get after it or it'll be in among the cavalry next and there'll be a flogging for you if that happens!"

Tom staggered to his feet, grabbed another musket and set off in pursuit of the Company's dinner to the cheers of his comrades.

He cornered the now foaming animal by a row of wooden huts. Officers' servants, grooms and horses were all around the huts and from the murmur of voices coming from the largest at the end there was some sort of conference in progress. Just as a clear voice rang out with, "What are you doing, my man?" Tom made a grab at the animal's tail.

The ox plunged off again but Tom hung on grimly, soon to be thrown off his feet and dragged through the dust. His musket went flying, discharging itself as it cracked against a stone. The terror-stricken animal then made straight for the large hut, crashing through the flimsy door and bringing down the whole building in a welter of beams, thatch, map tables and a crowd of very startled senior officers.

Tom ended up, still clutching the animal's tail, with a map round his head and a shiny black boot in his face. The whole camp came running to the scene, roaring with laughter and shouting encouragement.

With the animal trapped and soon led away, the officers dusted themselves down and assured each other they were little hurt. Hooper rushed up and dragged the bruised and bewildered Tom to his feet, frantically apologising to his superiors for the incident.

The senior Brigadier came out of the wrecked hut putting on his shako and trembling with laughter. "Shall I put him up for punishment, Sir?" asked Hooper.

"Damme, no! Funniest thing I ever saw. Man's got guts, sergeant. Did ye see how he clung on? Wouldn't give up, y' see. That's a good soldier. Damn my eyes, he deserves a drink!"

Tom looked around him with that bland expression he always assumed when he knew that once again he had got away with murder. A servant rushed up with glasses and a whisky decanter.

"Your health, soldier!" cried the brigadier. "I drink to your courage and tenacity and for giving me and my officers a damned good laugh!"

Tom took his glass and drained it at a gulp. "God bless your honour for them kind words. I can see you're a sportin' man, your Grace and I 'opes I has the pleasure o' fightin' alongside you soon. Would your honour like me to send a bit o' beef along for your servint to cook, for as soon as I've—"

"That'll do, Eagan," cut in Sergeant Hooper, knowing how Tom had a way of settling down as an orator; particularly when so rare a drink as whisky was to hand.

"I'm obliged to you, Sir for taking the incident in good part. I'll just get this man back to our lines for we've a meal to get over before sundown."

A flurry of salutes and goodnights and Eagan was led away by Sergeant Hooper through a line of cheering men from the 52nd. The Irishman had again provided a story that would be retold around many a bivouac fire.

Although plagued by flies, a merciless sun, shortage of rations and particularly water, the army preferred a summer campaign to the rigours of winter warfare. At times the days had an idyllic quality about them such as when they came to a stream or river and the whole affair took on the atmosphere of a country picnic.

The river banks would be lined with horses and cattle being watered, men filling casks and women washing clothes. The grime and sweat of a day's march would be washed away in large scale swimming and bathing sessions. The modesty of faraway England had long since left these men and women as they stripped and splashed around together with shrieks of laughter and much crude horse play.

As they plodded on towards the centre of Spain, the troops knew little and cared less of the disposition of the enemy. It was sufficient to worry about such things when the rumble of guns was heard. Yet strange rumours ran down the line that as the allied force was marching in one long straight line, the French were doing the same thing in parallel on the other side of a ridge to the left.

A gap in the ridge proved the rumour correct and a great buzz of excitement broke out at the sight of French colours, closely packed infantry with sunlight flashing from bayonets and swords.

The commander-in-chief and his staff had been aware of this position for days and also about a more worrying piece of intelligence concerning an approaching link up between two French armies. If this occurred Wellington would be at a numerical disadvantage and so with great reluctance he gave orders to prepare for a general withdrawal back into Portugal.

The men were furious at this, for to themselves they were invincible. As if to depress them further, that night produced a thunderstorm such as had never been experienced before in the Peninsular. Men and horses were struck by lightning, the horses breaking from picquet lines and causing wild stampedes through the huddled groups of soaking infantry.

Tom Eagan had acquired an umbrella from somewhere and squatted under its protection with a handful of veterans. One of them remarked that heavy rain was always an omen for a great battle. Wet and depressed, the troops hoped such a battle would start right now and Tom summed up for everybody with the remark that, "I'll be damned if the only way I can get dry would be to run about and kill a few Frenchmen."

By morning the clouds had rolled to the horizon to make a huge, white backdrop for the scene. A hot sun sent steam rising from the columns of men, horses and wagons, drying them out and leaving them refreshed and in high spirits. The parallel lines of march continued, with Wellington keeping his forces in compact groups while the French marshal, Marmont, allowed his larger army to string out.

During a halt the men munched biscuit and Wellington dismounted to rest his horse and gnaw away at a leg of cold chicken. A rearward movement of some baggage wagons caused dust clouds to rise, a fact carefully observed through telescopes by the French marshal and his staff. Misinterpreting this as being a general retreat by the British forces, the French made a great forward movement to cut off their enemy, a gap fast appearing between the forward French light troops and the main body.

Wellington was alert in a second, yelled for his telescope and saw his chance. "By God! That will do!" he shouted and hurled away the chicken bone. A stream of orders was given, horses mounted and the commander-in-chief himself rode like a madman to instruct personally his brother-in-law, Sir Edward Packenham.

The men cheered as they saw Wellington with flying coattails and attended by young Portuguese and British noblemen who, as ADCs, were hard pressed to keep up with their chief. Orders were scribbled on scraps of paper rested on a sabretache and, in flying dust, rumbling guns and the swinging into line of the long ranks of redcoats, the battle of Salamanca began.

For once the Light Division was not employed in the attack. In fact, to their great disgust, they were not called until nightfall and then only in the role of pursuit to try and head off the remains of a fast retreating French army.

But one event made a small piece of history for the 52nd Regiment, perhaps not to be recorded in memoirs or battle reports, but to be told with glee around soldiers' camp fires in the cool of the evening.

A number of baggage wagons had already been sent on the road back into Portugal, but Molly Eagan and her now close friend, Rosa, lingered behind with a rear party. Molly, who had lost or bartered away most of the loot she had won in previous actions was again on the lookout for what she called "bits an' pieces as takes me fancy", when the guns heralded the new battle.

She had long since lost her famous donkey; some said it died in protest at carrying her great weight. So slipping away from the rear lines of the Light Division she set off on foot in a flanking movement of her own to get near to the scene of battle and possible plunder.

This fat and fearless Irishwoman had seen so many of the sights of battle that she was unmoved by the rushing men, plunging, screaming horses and the thump and crash of artillery.

At home in Britain, men (to say nothing of women) would have fainted at the sight of this tough army wife sliding and loping her way forward past wounded and dead, smashed carts and all the debris of a swift action.

The British infantry had made several rapid charges along the flank of the French army and Wellington's dragoons had carried out one of the most spectacular cavalry charges of the war – a wild uncheckable dash through an entire enemy division with catastrophic results for the unfortunate foot soldiers.

The confusion of the late afternoon conflict grew worse and Molly halted on the edge of a ridge to take shelter in a small copse. She settled down to examine the contents of a pair of French haversacks.

With the background noises of the battle in her ears and her concentration on the rubbishy bits of loot in her lap, it is no wonder she did not notice the approaching line of eight French heavy dragoons. They were leading their horses, several of which had suffered slight cuts and injuries. The men themselves had lost their weapons and some their gorgeously plumed helmets. All looked tired, lost and dispirited until they saw the fat little Irishwoman.

At the first sight of them, Molly leapt to her feet, scattering her bits of plunder and turning to look for an escape route.

"B'God 'tis the Frenchy devils themselves! Now I'll be killed dead, sure I will and poor Tom'll never find me grave!"

The Frenchmen faced her in a half-circle, grinning wickedly and watching her with lusting eyes.

Molly, who had lived rough all her life and learned to size up situations quicker than most of her sex, realised that death was not likely to be her immediate fate. She saw at once that all of the men were unarmed and that their first reaction to her discovery was the natural one of good old-fashioned lust.

Well, that was fair enough and the prospect did not worry her nearly as much as it would have done a respectable housewife caught in such circumstances on her own doorstep. But eight of them was a formidable task for even such an easy-going woman as she.

The racket of the battle showed no sign of abating and even now musket balls whistled through the air around them and hoarse shouts could be heard just beyond the top of the ridge. The dragoons had a hurried conference and came to a unanimous decision.

Like all troops in action they were completely unaware of the overall battle situation and had some vague feeling that their own side was winning. It was logical therefore to get out of the fighting zone and back into the quieter regions of their rear area where they could enjoy their prize at more leisure.

The largest of their horses was brought forward and Molly, seized on all sides, was heaved into the saddle. In her inimitable way she broke into a giggle at the situation, but immediately covered her face with her hands and set up a pantomime of wailing and crying to make a suitable show of protest.

The party walked their mounts to the ridge and looked down on the slopes where all was still smoke and confusion. Wounded and dead lay all around, although the main part of the fighting had moved a few hundred yards to the north.

The dragoons mounted, the smallest of the men leaping up in pillion behind Molly and they cantered off to the edge of a wood where the French standards and groups of men indicated a rough and ready headquarters.

Instead of being congratulated at bringing in a female prisoner, the dragoons met a torrent of abuse from their comrades. An officer, with one arm in a bloodstained bandage and his beautiful uniform torn and stained with the fighting, waved a pistol at them and upbraided them for losing their arms and dallying with a British camp follower.

Molly dismounted and had the Frenchman's pistol thrust into her face. For a moment she thought this was now the end and she shut her eyes and fell on her knees for mercy.

In fact the great battle of Salamanca was already drawing to its close with a resounding victory for Wellington. This small group of mixed French cavalry and infantry was part of a divisional headquarters, now hurriedly preparing to join the general retreat of the whole of Marmont's army. If they wanted to survive the approaching night they would have to abandon all thoughts of dalliance with a plump Irish soldier's wife.

Opening her eyes a full minute later, Molly found herself in the ridiculous position on her knees with her captors already a dozen yards away and frantically burning papers, stores and packing essentials into saddlebags for a quick retreat.

She straightened up, regained her normal composure and looked around for a way out on her own terms. A line of horses was loosely tethered to some stunted trees and quickly she slipped the halter rope of the nearest of these. All around lay smashed carts, broken cannon, ammunition boxes and the usual debris of war, much of it blazing furiously. A pile of boxes, most of them split open, revealed the canvas bags of powder that charged the French guns.

She quickly grabbed two of these, ripping one open to make a rough and ready fuse. She tied the strips of canvas to the unopened bag, held it to a piece of burning wood and stood up like an Amazon with her improvised grenade.

The flame licked along the fuse in a couple of seconds and, judging the moment like a trained Fusilier, she hurled her missile at the packed group of Frenchmen as they bustled round their horses.

It was not so much an explosion as a gigantic flash of flame followed by an all-enveloping cloud of dense black smoke. As the powder bag flashed, Molly leapt with surprising agility for her bulk onto the back of the free horse. With a great shout she dug in her heels and went careering off in the opposite direction to the French retreat.

She cantered along for about ten minutes, shrieking with laughter at her escape and looking all around for some sign of her own people. She swept past parties out gathering up wounded and small sections reforming under officers and sergeants. All gave her a cheer as she passed.

Then on the other side of a small hill she saw the 52nd, still in line, still uncommitted to the battle. She charged down among them where they went mad with delight at the sight of their best known camp woman riding in on a French horse from the direction of the battle.

"—see lads, while we've stood here pickin' our noses, old Molly 'as been out an' dubbed the Frenchies on her own!"

"Have ye brought us back a present, Moll? A French cannon or suchlike?"

Tom and Jack broke ranks and came hurrying forward. "Where in the Devil have ye been, you great Clonmel cow?" shouted Tom. "I thought you was wid the wagons when a mate from the Connaughts wi' a bullet in his leg told me he saw you took!"

Molly pulled up her horse and aimed a blow at her man. "I've been to a party wi' the Frenchies but all they wanted was me on me back in a hay rick, so I blowed 'em all up wid a great big bomb and here I am an' roarin' for a drink!"

Jack helped her down from her horse with a quiet, "Good to see you back safe, Moll. Rosa was right alarmed when she heard they'd grabbed you. Did they get what they was after?"

"Did they Hell, Jack! Tho' 'twas a near thing at one moment. I was not so worried about that though; it was when a mad officer was goin' to shoot me I thought Old Moll was for joinin' them other poor devils lyin' out there."

Tom produced his usual secret bottle and Molly was soon restored to normal. A soldier led the French cavalry mount off to ingratiate himself with an officer by presenting it as a gift. Sergeant Hooper got his charges back in line and in the fading light they moved off to the flank of where the battle had developed into a rout of a French army.

At last the impatient Light Division was summoned up and sent at a cracking pace after the retreating French. But a disobedient Spanish officer, charged with guarding a vital bridge at Alba over the Torres River, had abandoned his post and the French streamed across to safety. The Light Division made a dash for a ford at Huerta but the bridge was the route for the French and nothing but a handful of stragglers and wounded were captured.

Wellington then reformed his army, manoeuvred up as far as Vallodolid; on hearing that King Joseph had the smallest of the French armies centred around the Spanish capital, he decided to act quickly and take the city before the other armies could come to the rescue of Napoleon's fat and incompetent brother.

As the men swung south the magic name "Madrid" passed down the delighted columns. Here was a prize to go for and they stepped out in their even more ragged uniforms and with battered wagons.

On a gloriously sunny day – August 12th, 1812 – the British Army of the Peninsular entered Madrid.

These were the occasions that became high watermarks in the soldiers' lives. They marched and fought and marched again. They endured terrible privations: starving, cold and wet, or burned with a merciless sun, they and their women took it all in their regular rhythmical stride. But, when a great city threw open its gates, the bells pealed, bands played and a hundred thousand Spaniards roared their welcome, the British soldier responded like a child given a great treat after a long and hard experience.

Wellington rode at the head of his troops, showered with flowers and garlands, his horse picking its way through a troop of ballet dancers who pirouetted in front. Houses were packed to the rooftops and gaily coloured carpets hung from windows, such things normally being reserved for a great religious festival.

Food and drink were offered in plenty, but strangely enough the troops who had drunk themselves into a state of raging savagery on so many occasions in the campaign now behaved with remarkable propriety.

Tom Eagan, smothered in flowers and eating a large water melon, remarked to his comrades. "This is the life, me boys! No more killin' and marchin' for me! I'll settle down and buy me a wine shop for this town'll do me 'til me old age."

Jack dug his friend in the ribs. "You'd not make a penny piece, Tom. You'd drink the profits as fast as they came in."

Tom grinned all round. "Ah! But 'twould be a marvellous, peaceful death for a poor old Irish soldier boy, would it not?"

King Joseph Bonaparte had foolishly left a small garrison manning the fortress of the Retiro in the city and Wellington set about dealing with this. A few regiments, including the 52nd, were detailed to sort out this minor irritation and the men formed up with enthusiasm and a desire to finish the job in double quick time and get at the flesh-pots of Madrid.

During the campaign Jack had reverted from time to time to his civilian trade of cobbler and in quiet times had often earned extra money by mending his comrades' shoes. With everybody trying to spruce themselves up for the city and their footwear never having been in a more worn state, Jack had been plagued to get his cobbler's kit in action and do a spot of patching.

Another regiment was being brought up so there was time to spare when Jack set up shop in the doorway of a small hut, laid out some strips of new leather they had found and banged away happily. A dozen men, including Hooper and Tom, flung their ragged shoes at him while Rosa poured cool mugs of white wine and praised his craftsman's skill.

An officer came up and Jack came to his feet. "I heard there was a cobbler among you and you must be the man," he cried. "Excellent! You can patch these old boots of mine while we're awaiting. Must look me best when we parade past His Lordship tomorrow."

Jack indicated an upturned cask. "Sit you down, Sir and let me have those off your feet. They'll be as good as new in minutes."

The reserve regiment stamped up into position. Men were ordered to the "stand-easy", pipes were lit and there was a general buzz of conversation about the sights of the great city. All was very peaceful until a cannon thumped out from the walls of the castle. The round shot whistled through the air and came crashing through the roof of Jack's hut in a shower of turf and timbers.

This was a signal for the waiting troops who leapt to their feet and ran through the gardens to attack the small fortress. Jack crawled from the wreck of the hut, covered in dust, and scattering shoes to right and left.

A dozen barefoot soldiers and an angry officer ran up, yelling for their footwear while bugles rang down the lines. "Where's me shoes, Wheeler...? I've only got one left footer... are we to go in barefoot? Sergeant!" The officer's boots were soon found and he sat down on the ground, red-faced and cursing, to tug them on. For the troops there was a moment of chaos while they tried to sort out their own shoes.

Some went forward with their feet slapping in sizes too large for them and others abandoned the search to run to the attack through flints and pebbles like bathers on a seashore. Jack rolled up his leather apron and tools, stuffed them in his knapsack and was off with his musket to the hoarse shouts of Sergeant Hooper urging his men into line.

A few sharp charges, some concentrated musket fire and the fort surrendered with only one of the attackers killed and two wounded.

Then the army really relaxed and set about the unaccustomed but attractive life of garrisoning a capital city.

They strolled in groups down the great wide street, buying sweetmeats, cooked meat and wine from the hundreds of stalls and booths that appeared to serve their needs. They went to bullfights, gazed at circus shows and played cards under the trees in the Prado.

Tom Eagan delighted a crowd of Madrilenos by catching some goldfish from a giant ornamental fountain and endeavouring to cook them over an improvised fire. The fish proved uneatable, but the entertainment developed into a near riot when Molly appeared on the scene, leading a donkey cart on which was perched a large barrel of wine. Eagan and his friends had the barrel tapped in seconds and jugs of the raw wine went the rounds of soldiers and civilians alike. The climax came when Tom, Molly and a handful of their comrades put on a hilarious, impromptu water carnival in the ornamental fountain.

While Molly splashed happily around, Tom was perched on the statuary in the centrepiece, anointing his wife from above with a large jug of wine.

Jack and Rosa settled down in the city like a long married couple. Prices everywhere were high, but Jack's share of odd pieces of loot was used to buy new clothes for his woman and to keep themselves well fed and housed.

Sitting on a bench in the city gardens one evening, with a bottle of wine and some cheese between them, Rosa took her man's hand into hers and gently told him that their child was on the way.

She had known she was pregnant for some time, but the recent battles, and the desire she maintained never to worry Jack about anything, had caused her to keep silent. The peaceful atmosphere of their life in Madrid seemed the perfect setting to reveal her secret, coupled with the fact that it was a situation that could not be concealed for very much longer.

Jack was overjoyed at the news and wanted to go in search of the Eagans and their other friends for a celebration party. But as they talked he slowly realised that bringing a child into their rough and tumble soldiers' life would be no picnic for Rosa, to say nothing of the chances of survival for the child. They settled down quietly together in each other's arms and planned for the future.

While the troops had their fill of the delights of Madrid, Wellington sent out his couriers and spies for information from the length and breadth of the Peninsular.

It was at this time the news reached him of Napoleon's great drive into Russia, where half a million men were sweeping all before them on the road to Moscow. This, coupled with the information that the French armies in Spain were again on the move and concentrating in ever large and menacing groups, made the prudent Wellington decide to move out of Madrid and head once more to the north.

The autumn days were upon them and if the commander was not to be trapped in an impossible defensive position with winter approaching, he must try and keep the initiative in his own hands.

Reluctantly the British marched out of the city and tramped along those dusty roads, with the leaves beginning to fall and those early morning mists having a sharp chill about them. It was back to work again and the sunny days of summer behind them.

Jack had bought a large, fur-lined coat for Rosa and a pair of knee-length soft leather boots lined with wool. He fussed and bothered around his now plump girl, anxious for her comfort and worried sick that winter would be at its height when her time came.

September and October passed, with the abortive action at Burgos and the allied troops continuing to manoeuvre within a tightening circle of French armies. It was in mid-November that Wellington realised he must retreat, get his tired and ragged army into winter quarters.

They set off in the lowest of spirits, back over familiar roads across Castile and heading for the bleak hills of Portugal. On the day the retreat started, the winter rains set in. For all the triumphs of the 1812 campaign, this was the low watermark for Wellington's army.

The cold rain splashed down under the force of a driving wind. Rivers and streams were soon in flood and came roaring down the hillsides and across the line of march. Roads became quagmires and the soaked and sickened troops bent their heads to the storm and lurched on in a blind fury. The icy mud sucked boots and shoes from their feet and swaying ox-drawn baggage wagons were constantly in trouble, needing squads of men to heave them on their way.

To add to all this, there had been a commissariat blunder and the army's rations were sent on ahead by another route. For four pitiful days the troops added hunger to their frozen and wet condition.

A captain in the Rifles had his sick brother with him and supported him on a near dead mule, never once leaving his side. Dysentery and the ague struck with terrifying speed and the wagons were stripped of surplus stores to be piled with sick men along with the huddled women.

On the second day the famished troops saw a herd of pigs blunder out of a forest to their front. Bayonets flashed and the air was full of squealing. For a few hundred at the head of the columns it was pork for dinner that night. For the bulk of the army it was acorns, fragments of dried beef and water.

Jack, Tom and their immediate friends congregated around Molly's ox cart and either hung on to its side to keep themselves going or pushed with sudden bursts of energy when the wagon became completely stuck in the glutinous mud.

Jack stayed near the tailboard of the cart and was forever enquiring how Rosa felt. She was huddled in a bundle of soaking blankets, but was at least protected from the wind by the fur coat and boots they had so prudently bought in the sunny days at Madrid.

Molly Eagan, looking more ragged and dirty than ever before, lurched to the back of the cart. "Stop your worriting, Jack Wheeler," she cried. "Haven't she got me to look to her and see she's well. Sure I've had more children than you've fired your musket and some of those I've had on the side o' the road. I've a drop o' good rum here what Tom thieved from a sargint and that'll keep the cold out o' me an' Rosa 'til we can get a bit o' fire goin' an' a drop of good soup on the boil!"

The retreat continued for four days and nights, spurred on by the harassing of the French cavalry. Hundreds dropped out to be scooped up as prisoners or to die on the roadside from cold and exhaustion.

The worst job was given to the Light Division who formed the rearguard and had the double task of helping and urging forward those troops who still had a spark of life in them and periodically halting to fire volleys back at the French when they came within range.

It was a sad and tattered army that dragged itself into Ciudad Rodrigo and across the frontier to Almeida. But here was shelter, food and warmth and the men drew on their last reserves of energy to get into billets, gather fuel and collect rations before collapsing in heaps on beds, in cow sheds or on the bare boards of empty houses.

Jack and Tom lifted Rosa carefully from a cart while Molly kicked in the door of a large stone house in Almeida. A bed was set up in the front room and a fire was soon roaring up the chimney place. Molly bustled about like a woman possessed, issuing orders to all and sundry, getting the house straight, food in the cook-pots and distributing her menfolk and their friends about the house like Wellington deploying his armies.

The rains turned to snow and the troops seldom ventured beyond their own front doors except to draw rations or turn out as sentries.

On a bitterly cold night just before Christmas, Rosa turned on her side and gave Jack a sound thump on his head. "Jack, Oh Jack! Get Molly now—I think the baby come—be quick—pains are here…!" She broke off into a series of heavy grunts as Jack rolled out of bed and groped around the floor for a candle.

He blew on the embers of the fire to get a flame for his candle then staggered off into the next room where Tom and Molly were snoring heavily under a heap of army blankets, sheepskins and old rugs.

"Moll! Moll!" he shouted, shaking the fat Irishwoman until she heaved herself up and sent her sleeping partner crashing out of the bed to the floor. "Moll," cried Jack, "Rosa's in labour. The baby's coming. 'Tis coming now, for sure. Please get to her quickly, for it's woman's work now."

Molly heaved herself out of the bed and flung a large Spanish cloak round her shoulders. "Quit your blatherin' Jack. We'll have hours to wait yet, you see if I'm not right. Get into the kitchen an' have a good fire goin' with a pot o' boiling water when I'm ready. Get to that chest o' mine in the corner there for I've a heap of good clean linen that we'll need for this job."

She stumbled about and trod on her recumbent husband who had remained sleeping in spite of the sudden change from warm bed to draughty floor. "Now what's this down here? Is it a weasel I've trod on? Wake up, me beauty, for if I'm to lose me sleep I shall want a bit o' company with it."

"What! Ho! The devil's horns!" cried Tom. "Is it the French come upon us?"

Molly pulled her spouse to his feet where he stood like a tattered scarecrow in a weird collection of night-clothes consisting of a Spanish lady's dress, a French cavalry coat and a woollen night-cap, the last item stolen from a British officer.

"It's Jack here," said Molly, "come from Rosa where the baby's startin' its little tricks an' wants to come out into the cold hard world. If it knew what it was in for, it would stay right there all cosy an' warm an' not come an' join us lot o' wanderin' vagabonds."

"The baby, eh!" cried Tom. "Well here's a thing an' me wid not a drop o' liquor in the house to drink the little creater's health. I'm off to where I know I can get a spot o' something to wish the wee morsel well an' cheer us all up at the same time."

Molly bustled off and Jack went to the next house for the assistance of a sergeant's wife, reputed to be well versed in the problems of child bed.

Tom scrambled into his trousers and greatcoat and set off through the snow swinging an oil lantern on one of his instinctive searches for a bottle.

Fires were banked up, water boiled and Jack sat biting his fingers in the kitchen while cries and muffled noises came from the front bedroom. Tom was soon back, shaking the snow from his boots and brandishing a full bottle of Scotch whisky that had been liberated from a very senior officer's store cart.

Before the would-be father and his friend had disposed of a half of the bottle, Molly came into the kitchen and proudly presented Jack with a tiny, bawling, red faced creature. "Here ye are, m'lad. A son. A lovely little son for you an' Rosa and she doin' fine in there."

Jack turned to the grinning Tom, took a gulp at his glass and grabbed a candle to get a closer look at the squirming, wizened little face.

"Well, by God Moll! Tom! Isn't that a great thing! A son! By heaven—a son! Hold him careful, Molly. Is he warm enough? Make that fire up, Tom! Get some clean wraps for him! By God, this is a great moment!"

He staggered past them and into the front bedroom. By the light of only two candles the room looked like the corner of a battlefield. But a smiling, sweat-stained Rosa was lying back on her pillows and held up a hand to her man.

He knelt beside her, kissed her gently and then slowly wiped her face with a towel. The sergeant's wife cleaned up in the background while the happy man murmured a mixture of thanks, prayers and endearments to the now contented woman.

Next morning the news spread around the billets of the 52nd and all day a procession of friends and their wives called - some with little presents, some with odd bottles for a celebration drink and all with offers of help if needed.

The winter passed on to the first glimpses of spring. The news of Napoleon's disaster in Russia brought new heart to the army in Spain and Wellington became impatient for the roads to clear, the sun to shine and to be off to finish the French once and for all.

Somewhat belatedly, tents were issued to the soldiers. The old heavy iron kettles were replaced with light ones made of tin such as each soldier could carry with his kit. Three new pairs of shoes were issued to every man, new blankets and – because of the tents – greatcoats were discarded.

A medical corps under a brilliant surgeon set to work reorganising the hospitals and many sick men were returned to health and service with their regiments.

Reinforcement transports sailed daily from England and disembarked their raw cargo of "Johnny Newcomes" at Lisbon to follow the road that Jack and Tom had taken two long years before.

As they came up to join the main army they found that same sharp contrast; the new men white of face and dressed in smart, clean uniforms and the veterans tanned like old leather, clad in faded, patched clothing and wearing the expression of men who knew what was to be done when the bands struck up and the colours unfurled into the first sunshine of spring.

CHAPTER NINE

Now All You Young Soldiers

The old familiar pattern again: the kit packed, the sergeants shouting, bands playing and colours aloft at the head of each column of marching men.

Wellington now commanded 52,000 British troops. In addition he had 29,000 well trained, equipped and disciplined Portuguese. He and his army were never more fit, never in better heart.

The new boys picked up the step from the veterans. They learned the songs of the march, the way to make a bivouac in a few minutes, to stretch their rations when the commissariat was late and to feast like kings when the cook-pots were full.

Skirmishes and minor battles were taken in the stride of this invincible army sweeping across Northern Spain. Fantastic feats of military engineering were performed to the delight of their ambitious commander. Rivers were crossed in no time by skilfully rigged pontoon bridges that travelled with the head of the force on specially built horse-drawn wagons, mounted on artillery wheels. The slow ox carts with their wide, flat wheels were being abandoned for these faster transports, particularly for the bridging boats and heavy military stores.

At the end of May and again in early June, the army tackled what seemed to be impassable mountains where the infantry climbed on their hands and knees. On both these occasions the guns were lowered over precipices by ropes with their wheels locked and manhandled by sweating gunners and cursing infantry.

Jack kept in constant touch with the baggage train to watch over his Rosa and their tiny son. Molly was in attendance on the child and would send poor Tom on endless foraging expeditions for "—a bit o' lean goat's meat for me to boil some broth for the little lad," or "—stir your lazy legs, Tom Eagan, an' get down to that farm, for we're runnin' short o' fresh milk for the poor wee mite!"

As foraging came naturally to the Irishman, he never failed on the many searches his wife sent him and often came back with a bonus of eggs, butter and fresh vegetables.

Sometimes the shorter mountain routes taken by the troops would separate them from the rear parties and stores wagons for several days. When they linked up again, Jack would rush through the divisional lines at the first sight of the baggage column, leap up on the cart and grab his son from his smiling girl to dance back and forth with the child.

Around the nightly fire with food and wine inside them, the Wheelers and the Eagans would sit like old neighbours on a communal porch. All around would be the coming and going of troops in the flickering firelight - raucous and bawdy laughter in one corner of a field, a guitar and soft singing in another.

On one such a night in the Light Division's lines the famous Rifles – the 95th – were roaring out their usual song, *I'm Ninety Five, I'm Ninety Five and very glad to be alive …!* In a corner under the shade of the wagon, Jack was heaping more wood on the fire when Tom leaned across and took the child from Rosa.

"Now you daft clown," cried Molly. "Be careful with that infant, he's not a bottle o' rum you know!"

"Sure an' don't I love the little fella like he was me own and I'd fight to me death if anyone came near to harm him. I was just feelin' like singin' him a little song – a soldier's song for a soldier's lad."

"I think he's drunk early tonight," said Molly to Rosa, but Tom ignored her as he cradled the child in his arms and softly crooned one of the oldest and most popular of the Peninsular songs.

> Now all you young soldiers
> Come list to my story,
> For the shilling you took
> Won't bring you much glory.
>
> Don't squander your money
> On girls from the city,
> For the girls from the city
> Are no use to you.

Rosa had tears in her eyes as she took the sleeping child back to her bosom. She was not a great talker except when alone with Jack; although her English had improved enormously from the halting phrases at their first meeting. But she felt the occasion demanded a short speech. "A good song, Tom. A song for my little boy. You both such good friends to Jack and me. You do so many kind things for me and my little one. I love you both—Molly and Tom."

"Now isn't that nice?" said Tom. "I'll drink your health on it, so I will."

He dived behind the cart to produce a bulging goatskin of wine and they all had their tin mugs full in a moment. It was not until the fire had died down to a heap of dull embers that they crawled into their tents. Jack felt as happy as at any time of the campaign and he laid blankets out on a bed of soft ferns and carefully placed the baby on a sheepskin between himself and his dear Rosa.

Wellington piled up the pressure on the French army in the north. To the south the other French armies were heavily engaged in a bitter, no-quarter struggle with hordes of Spanish guerrillas.

King Joseph Bonaparte himself, with Marshal Jourdan, had halted his 58,000 force around the city of Vitoria. Although a formidable army, the fat, incompetent and pleasure-loving brother of the emperor had a further 20,000 souls under his charge. But these were a hindrance rather than a help to his hard-pressed troops. They were a vast horde of courtiers, servants, wives, camp followers, actresses, ballet companies and courtesans; all taking up space, all requiring food and the whole lot spread over several miles of road in more than 5,000 carriages, wagons and carts.

By the middle of June the British were poised for attack and King Joseph's army was as ripe a piece of fruit as any they had picked in Spain. Rations had been short again in the British ranks, this time for five days past. As the redcoats fixed their flints they said they could smell the frog-eaters' baccy and onions.

A famished Tom turned to Jack and cried, "My stomach's yellin' out for a bite o' food Jacko. We must either fall in with the commissariat or the French today—I care not which!"

On the 21st of June, Wellington brought them into line for a series of convergent and encircling attacks on the enemy. There were delays and some confusion among the main attacking forces, but the incredible Light Division made a silent crossing of the Zadorra river and were soon joined by their old comrades of the Third. Tough veteran, General Picton, was there, calling to his men, "Come on, ye rascals! Come on, ye fighting villains!"

They fired, charged and fired again, leaping over hedges and ditches, rushing through standing corn and driving the French from the shelter of farmyards and small villages.

King Joseph's men were in ideal country for defence and by all the rules of war should have driven the British back. But they were tired after their long retreat before the relentless Wellington and many were dispirited at the thought of each backward step bringing them nearer to the frontier and their own country.

The throwing away of arms began as a trickle and developed into a flood. Looking over their shoulders the French caught the smell of panic and they fled in their thousands. Guns were abandoned as the artillery horses were cut from the traces and seized to speed the rout. Marshal Jourdan and King Joseph mounted such horses and joined in the wild retreating tumult, taking nothing but the clothes they rode in and the unfortunate marshal losing his gold and jewel-studded baton in the confusion.

If the marshal lost a baton, the King and his court lost very much more.

Just beyond Vitoria on the narrow road to Pamplona the British and Portuguese came upon a sight that momentarily stopped them in their tracks. Then, in spite of Wellington's fury, his soldiers plunged into the fantastic lines of carriages and carts and went on the biggest looting spree that has ever been the lot of an army in the field. All thought of pursuit was lost in the turmoil that followed.

The fast approaching darkness caused hundreds of flares and lanterns to be lit and the scene became one gigantic fairground.

Carriages were overturned and the screaming occupants scattered like the chickens, goats and cattle that were already inextricably mixed up in the confusion. Fires were lit everywhere, many from the woodwork of smashed carts and carriages or the beautiful pieces of furniture that were scattered around. Booths were set up and troops opened shop with jugs of wine to hand and cries of "Who'll give me fifty dollars for this gold clock?" or "Three fine paintings of the gentry and a silver bird cage for a bonus an' all for a hundred dollars!"

Cases and boxes were split open by hurling them from the top of the carriages and the redcoated infantry trampled around in a profusion of silks and fine clothes, china and silver tea services, chalices and church ornaments and ten thousand other items the result of six years' acquisition by Joseph's court.

Tom Eagan was at the head of the rush with Molly close behind him. He stripped off his tattered clothes and appeared on the roof of a general's carriage dressed from head to foot in the owner's best ceremonial uniform. The fact that the French general must have been a man of over six feet tall and of proportionate build only increased the comic appearance of the little Irishman.

"Get down out o' that!" screamed Molly. "There's work to be done! Gi' me a hand wi' these small boxes for by their weight there's money in them!"

Shrewd Molly had sensed that the plundering and eating of masses of rich food, the picking up and swapping of gewgaws or awkward-to-conceal silks and paintings was all good fun but paid poor dividends in the long run. Money, preferably gold coin, was an investment for the future, an insurance against many more hard days to come. Besides, she had no illusions about the tough life that lay ahead for she and Tom, even if they survived the campaign and returned to their homeland.

The Irishwoman was one of the first to discover that lockers were built in under the seats of many of the carriages. A quick blow from an axe and the wrenching out of a few planks would often reveal small mahogany and brass bound boxes with locks of fine workmanship. A further attack with the axe on the beautiful woodwork produced leather bags of gold francs, dollars, doubloons, Louis d'Ors and a score of other currencies, all of them very portable and negotiable.

Tom and Jack set to under Molly's direction and formed a relay of bearers back to their baggage wagon with French soldiers' knapsacks packed and heavy with coin.

Rosa put her sleeping child on a heap of blankets and carefully stowed the loot in different hiding places around the big wagon.

Wellington's officers, sent in to quell the riot, and get the troops back for an early start next morning, were themselves tempted by the scenes of plunder and in the semi-darkness many of them emptied their saddlebags of kit and iron rations and filled them with more valuable stores.

Tom and Molly, engaged in unloading a pile of stout boxes from a service wagon were startled to find themselves under the scrutiny of Sir James Kempt, commander of one of the brigades in the Light Division. Accompanied by an ADC, bearing a lantern, the senior officer strode forward and demanded of the Irishman, "What have you there, my man?"

"Sure an' if it isn't Sir James himself. God bless your honour! Wasn't I just sorting out a few things for just such an officer as you, Sir? Here's all the fine things King Joseph has left us for our hard day's work, all free, gratis and for nothin'. Would your honour like a drink?"

He produced a silver and cut glass decanter of fine brandy but was brushed aside with, "Never mind about that. Go and find me a pack mule and load these boxes for me. I must get them back to the headquarters chest!"

Tom grabbed a mule and he and Molly set about loading the boxes with the assistance of the ADC. When the skinny animal's back was near breaking under the weight, Sir James ordered his officer to set out for headquarters and await his return.

"Here, soldier!" he cried. "There's a box left over. You may do as you wish with it for your trouble, but if it's found in your kit tomorrow you know you may be forced to hand it over. That's your affair—goodnight to you."

The Brigadier rode off after his pack mule and

Molly exploded in a torrent of abuse for what she called, "the interferin' varmint!"

"I'm not distressed meself," said Tom. "We've a good haul stashed away already and there's plenty o' the night left yet."

Molly broke open the remaining box and held a flickering candle over the contents. She shrieked with laughter and fell back rolling on the ground.

Jack joined them at that moment, having come from helping Rosa with their last consignment of loot. "Now what's old Molly found that's so funny?" he asked of Tom.

Tom was peering into the box himself when he too let out a shout of laughter. "God split me breeches!" he cried. "An' I thought it was all gold by the weight o' them boxes. Horseshoes an' nails! Horseshoes an' nails for Sir James Kempt himself an' his precious officers. I hope he gives a few crates to Sir Arthur as a present. Oh, my eye! Who says there ain't justice for a poor soldier?"

The three friends worked steadily but were now finding the money boxes harder to find. Food and drink came next on their list of requirements and Molly soon had her wagon crammed with good things for the future, including a dozen crates of live and noisy chickens.

Tom and Jack, leaving the womenfolk to sorting and packing, went back once more into this large scale Donnybrook Fair. By now the place was roaring with the biggest carousel of the Peninsular War.

In one corner of a field a company of ballet dancers and actresses had been forced to set up their travelling stage and scenery to put on a show for the victorious troops. The frightened women in their flimsy costumes danced and paraded, singing in nervous voices that were drowned by the hoarse shouts and drunken cries of their audience.

The show came to an abrupt end when a tipsy fool upset a cask of brandy at the side of the stage, dropped a lighted torch in the confusion and the scenery was soon ablaze from end to end.

The panic-stricken performers leapt from the stage into the welcoming arms of the delighted and cheering redcoats, there to be borne off in triumph to dark corners of the field, to upturned carriages and other secret places for a different kind of entertainment.

All through the night the fires blazed and the troops ate, danced, sang, made love or lurched about in a stupor until a pale dawn saw those that could stagger make their way back to their lines. They left behind a smoking ruin of what had been the baggage train of Joseph Bonaparte, puppet King of Spain.

An angry Wellington put in his despatches to Lord Bathurst in London a remark that, "…my rascals have got among them upwards of a million in sterling, with the exception of 100,000 dollars, which were got for the military chest."

Parades were called and kit laid out to reveal any plunder, but little came to light. There were such sights as two soldiers leading a protesting mule while they balanced on its back a large wooden bed, complete with blankets and bedclothes. One soldier came into his regimental area with a fine white tablecloth which he had seized in one go, scooping up plates, silver, cutlery and all. He laid this out and sorted breakages from the debris, then proceeded to entertain his comrades at breakfast.

Hospitals had to be set up for the wounded and the thousands of French camp followers; wives and children put into billets and issued with rations and clothing.

While his staff worked like beavers, Wellington was impatient for his divisional commanders to get their men into some semblance of fighting order and set off for Pamplona and the retreating enemy.

Through heavy summer rains alternating with blazing hot days the army got on the move into the northern extremities of the Peninsular.

Marshal Soult, known to the British infantry as "old salt!" had taken command of the demoralised French soldiers and fought hard but unsuccessful actions all the way up into the Pyrenees.

Pamplona was surrounded and put to the siege. A series of sharp encounters took place at Sorauen, San Sebastian, on the coast by the frontier, and the mountain passes at Maya and Roncevalles. With the French withdrawing all along the Pyrenees and San Sebastian surrendering after fierce fighting on the last day of August, Wellington was poised to sweep his enthusiastic troops down on to the soil of France.

As another autumn came upon them the British harried and harassed the French wherever they halted to give battle.

News reached Wellington of the Austrians joining the alliance, committing themselves with Russia and Prussia to drive at Napoleon from the north while Wellington's veterans pushed up from the south into France.

Strangely enough the British were welcomed by the French peasants and the inhabitants of the small towns in that south-western corner of France.

Napoleon had bled his country of men and money and the population were sick of every aspect of this war that seemed never ending.

The British were ordered to behave with correctness and discipline towards the local people. Wellington could not afford men to guard long lines of communication and keep supply routes open. When they came to pay for billets, forage and stores, the French civilians welcomed them like heroes and liberators. The French troops, used to the system of living off the country in Spain and Portugal, tried the same tactics as they withdrew into their own country. In return they were treated with a sullen contempt and as little co-operation as possible.

The winter set in hard, the coldest in Europe for many years, with roads made frequently impassable by snow or heavy rain.

Wellington had kept the pressure of engagement on the French until the very end of 1813. Then the weather put a brake on even his enthusiasm and his half-frozen but still lively troops took shelter for the first six weeks of the new year.

In mid-February an unexpected fine spell of weather enabled the roads to dry out and the British were off again.

A siege force was sent to surround and threaten Bayonne, while the commander-in-chief himself led his main army to attack the river lines that branched from the River Adour into five fingers of snow torrents.

The bridges of boats were hauled up again and one after the other the river obstacles were crossed.

On the morning of the 27th February, the Light Division, together with the 3rd, 4th, 6th, and 7th, had crossed the Gave de Pau and were facing the French. The latter were stretched in an L-shaped formation with their right extremities on the town of Orthez.

The French guns thundered and flashed along the entire front and a lot of shot went over the heads of the waiting redcoats and into the river behind them.

In the kneeling-before-attack position the 52nd primed their muskets and fixed their flints. Tom passed his usual bottle around his nearest comrades and chatted as he always did before action.

"I hope nobody's splashin' over that river now, for I'm thinkin' it's mighty hot back there."

Sergeant Hooper took the bottle for a swig and replied, "Ay, Tom! Hot enough. But thank God there's nobody there. The reserves is across and lying low just to our rear."

Jack sat quietly with that tense feeling that even the veterans had before a charge, yet still as confident as ever that he would not be killed. He turned to Tom and grinned. "Y'know Tom, we've seen a power of fights these last few years and I'm keen to get these Frenchies on the run to Paris itself. With that lad of mine growing so fast it's time we got our bounty and set sail for old England. If this damned war goes on much longer, we'll be signing him on in the 52nd and he'll be soldiering along of us."

"You're right, to a nail," said Tom. "If it goes on so long as your lad's a joinin' up then I'll be a shivering old fool wid a white beard an' Molly will have to hold me muskit still while I fires it."

"Did you see how far back our wagons lay?" called Jack to Sergeant Hooper.

"They're just lying beyond the river," replied the sergeant. "They'll be over soon enough if we clear this little lot to our front and you'll get your hot bacon and a kiss from that woman of yours."

"Ah! There's a woman," said Tom. "There's a beauty for you. If I'd come over without that great lass o' mine an' old Wheeler here hadn't tipped his hat the first night we landed, I might 'ave 'ad a go there meself!"

Hooper moved across to join the conversation. "You're a lucky devil, Wheeler," he said, "but you're a good soldier and you deserves a good woman. Was you thinking of marrying her if we get out of this war with all our limbs straight?"

"Yes I was," said Jack. "Marry her soon as I can, tho' it will have to be in a Catholic church with all the ceremonies and suchlike. We're English Protestants back home and I can't see our old parson taking kindly to me marching up his churchyard with a bride on one arm and a bouncing boy in the other."

Tom rocked with laughter. "Come to Ireland wid Molly an' me. We'll get you married in a Catholic church wid all the blessin' o' the Pope 'imself an' I'll be your sponsor and Molly will attend on Rosa. We could have a weddin' party to last a week!"

His eyes shone with the thought of it all. Hooper turned his head as they heard bugles sounding in the distance and to their right. A cluster of senior officers came cantering into view.

A rattle of musket fire and the hoarse cheering of troops on the charge meant the attack had begun on the right. The senior officers halted at the rear of the Light Division and the men broke into roar upon roar of cheering as they recognised "Our Arthur", Wellington himself, directing each stage of the battle and personally giving the order to attack.

A few shouted commands, an imperious pointing gesture with a telescope from the dark clad mounted figure and the Light Division was on its feet and away like demons with the 52nd in the lead.

Straight up a narrow valley with a Roman camp at the end and under a hail of French musketry the troops plunged and reared forward. The 52nd was ordered to jink left in an independent action and take the village and church of St Boes.

"Come on, the 52nd!" roared their commander, Sir Charles Alten. "Come on, for Sir Arthur himself has asked for you today! He's watching you men, so go at it!"

Their skirmishes ran as though after a fox, leaping over obstacles and firing, reloading, and firing like men possessed. The main formation kept a tight shape and poured terrible volleys at the packed French infantry. So close did skirmishers and battalion keep and so fast did they fire to their front, the French thought they were being attacked by a tidal wave.

Other parts of the battle had not gone well until the 52nd crashed through its opposition and turned the tide for Wellington. After they had cut the French army in two the remainder of the British forces spurred themselves on to write another chapter of success for their commander. Orthez went into the military histories with particular reference to "the swift and majestic advance of the fighting 52nd".

Drenched with sweat and powder-blackened as usual, the troops halted and watched a tiny cloud of retreating French soldiers disappear into the twilight, again hurling their weapons from them in panic.

A mass of wounded had to be picked up and most of this work was organised by the British and carried out by over a thousand French prisoners. The 52nd was formed up by the bugle calls and set to escorting prisoners and wounded to the rear.

During the last stages of the battle a spent musket ball struck Wellington on his sword hilt, driving it against his thigh. Although the wound was slight, it put the commander out of action for several days - the only such time in all his years in the Peninsular.

Back in the valley the troops were joined by their rear parties and wagons. Fires were lit, lanterns hung around and everybody felt in great heart after another day of hard work.

The prisoners stood in shivering, miserable groups, hoping for a morsel of food from their conquerors before being sent marching to the rear. Some of the captives were mere boys, last minute conscripts with the minimum of training and thrust into a line to oppose the hardened veterans of Wellington's army.

One such was a lad of barely seventeen, dressed in an ill-fitting uniform but without shoes. He sobbed quietly after the shock of the battle and the disgrace at finding himself a prisoner. He moved away a few paces from his comrades and stared around in the flickering firelight like a trapped animal. He found himself by a working party of sentries, loading and priming muskets for their night rounds.

He grabbed one of the loaded arms and slipped silently behind a tree, unnoticed in the semi-darkness and the general bustle of camp.

General Alten, Commander of the Light Division, was standing in the centre of a group of men, silhouetted by a blazing fire. The general had just accepted a glass of wine from Sergeant Hooper and was toasting his men for their victory at Orthez. The young prisoner saw the cocked hat and the glimmer of gold braid. Perhaps this was the great Wellington, the scourge of the French.

In a blind fury he raised the musket and pulled the trigger. The explosion was followed by a split second of silence as the badly aimed ball whistled through the air towards the ring of baggage wagons. A single, short scream and Rosa Silvero pitched headlong from the top of her wagon to fall at the feet of a thunderstruck Jack and Molly.

Everything then happened in a few seconds. Jack crashed down beside his woman and in agony turned her over in his arms. Molly leaped to the side of the cart and grabbed the lantern, calling for help from all around her.

Tom went like a whirlwind in the direction of the shot and his quick eyes saw the white and frightened face of the youth and the still smoking musket. Although other soldiers ran to the prisoner, Tom was there first. With an expression of hatred such as none had ever seen on his face before, even in the thick of their fiercest battles, the Irishman made a rush for the young man, raised a bayonet and struck once— straight for the heart. He turned away immediately as the youth collapsed in death, leaving him to the others to drag from under the trees and into the light of a fire.

Tom strode silently back to the wagon where all was now in turmoil. Sir Charles had summoned his surgeon who came running with two assistants and a pannier of medical equipment. A ring of lanterns was already forming around Molly who screamed her orders for more light, blankets, sheets, a bed, anything to render assistance for the Portuguese girl. But, down on the ground, a shaking Jack had already felt the blood seeping through Rosa's dress just above the heart and frantically bent to her face to listen for a sign of life. She had coughed twice when he first seized her, had murmured something in Portuguese. But now there was silence and as more lanterns brightened the scene he could tell that calm but rigid set in her beautiful face and the stillness of all her limbs meant this was the end of Rosa Silvero, dancer from Albergaria and Lisbon and loyal woman to a soldier of the Peninsular.

Jack was dragged away by his comrades while the surgeon and his assistants made a brief examination. As the officer straightened up, he shook his head to the circle of men and women. He murmured something to his orderlies about smashed ribs, damaged heart and almost instant death.

The hardened soldiers who had seen death so many times were now deeply moved. Their womenfolk wept openly.

Tom joined Molly who had a large arm around the silent and wildly staring Jack. The Irishman poured some brandy into a tin mug, gave it to Jack who took a few sips. As Jack dropped the mug he suddenly stiffened. "The man! The man who fired! Where is he? I must get…" he cried out.

"It's all over, Jacko lad," said Tom, quietly. "All over now. 'Twas a young fool of a Frenchy; mad, I reckon. I've killed him 'an they're buryin' him now. Sit you down a bit an' rest. Ah! A sad night for all of us, so it is."

Molly, dry eyed but very tense, brought a chair and forced Jack into it. The man sat with drooping head, muttering odd phrases about his dead woman; her name, the Volera dance, Badajoz, Lisbon and a jumble of half-forgotten memories.

Sergeant Hooper had been at work with his usual efficiency and had ordered some of the women to prepare Rosa's body for burial. A volunteer working party had chosen a quiet spot by a cypress tree and were already digging the grave.

In the midst of all this a sudden cry of a child came from the top of the baggage wagon. "Holy Mary, pray for us all for we's all forgot the little fella," muttered Molly as she climbed up to gather the Wheeler child in her arms.

Tom helped her down with unusual tenderness and she stood holding the child in front of Jack. "There now, Jack," she said quietly. "There's a kind of fate in all this for you've somethin' left to take home. There's still the lad what's the spit image o' poor Rosa and you've plenty to do keepin' him from harm."

She went to hand the child to him but he pushed her back. "You, Molly. You look to him for me. He needs a mother still. Look to my lad for me and leave me to myself."

As Molly and Tom slithered into an untidy tent and lay the child between them, they left outside the hunched figure of a sad and weary soldier, silhouetted against the fading light of a camp fire.

At dawn Rosa was buried with a larger than usual attendance of mourners for such an occasion. A Portuguese priest, travelling with the Cacadores of the Light Division had read the office and Sir Charles

Alten had turned out with some of his officers. Hooper on one side and Tom on the other supported a grim faced Jack as the blanket-covered body was lowered into the grave.

Carpenters from the bridging train had worked during the night to fashion a stout wooden cross on which Rosa's name had been burned with a hot iron.

Later in the day the Battalion and Division marched off again, deeper into the wide plains of southern France and with a fiercely maternal Irishwoman clutching a gurgling child as she straddled the top of her wagon.

One more major battle faced the tough and wiry veterans of Spain – Toulouse. In early April, through conditions of some of the worst mud the army had ever met, Wellington led his hardened warriors forward to take the pro-Royalist city by storm. The wagons and siege guns had a terrible time getting through the swampy clay of the approaches and even the Commander's light coach, which he seldom used, required four mules, four draft horses and two oxen to drag it through the axle deep mire.

The troops slithered and splashed forward, cursing the conditions and the enemy alike. Jack, who had spoken very little since the loss of his Rosa, was suddenly seized with a fury and abandon that frightened those around him.

Hooper and Tom called out to him as he charged in with a pack of skirmishers at a tightly held French palisade.

"Get back, Wheeler!" cried the sergeant. "Get back to the square and reload! Leave that to the Rifles, 'til we charge proper!"

"He's fightin' mad, I reckon," shouted Tom. "He don't seem to care 'bout himself no more since she were killed. Look at the wild bastard! We'll be diggin' his grave 'fore nightfall at this rate!"

A group of skirmishers had pulled out part of the French defensive palisade and a fierce hand to hand fight was taking place barely fifty yards from the halted main infantry. Jack had got in with the Rifles and some men of the Connaughts, and, using his musket as a club, was flailing about him like a madman.

The bugles sounded and the waiting troops rose to a man and rushed into the position, firing as they ran. A breathless, somewhat battered Wheeler was soon surrounded by his comrades.

"You're a right fool, Jacko!" shouted Tom as he came up beside his friend. "I thought you was down a score o' times. Look to yourself now, and remember that kid o' yours. This war's nigh over an' who wants to get a bullet in his guts when we might all be home 'fore long?"

Jack grinned and mopped a gash on his forehead. He thumped his friend on the back as they set off to round up prisoners. "You're right, Tom. You're always a right little cuss and knows what's what in this game. I suddenly thought of poor Rosa and wanted to kill all those bastards with me bare hands. But I'm thinking the end's in sight now, so it's care and attention from now on for Jack Wheeler and a safe passage home."

The entry of the British into the city of Toulouse was not unlike the triumphal march into Madrid. The troops were astonished that their enemy of yesterday should welcome them as liberators. But Toulouse was strongly Royalist in its sympathies and hated the Napoleonic regime and all that had gone with it.

As the mud-stained British redcoats in threadbare uniforms and with shot-ridden colours marched down the main boulevards they were showered once more with garlands and presents, wine and food. The cheers of the ladies from the balconies drowned the music of their own bands.

That very evening, while Wellington's men had a high old time in the city, a dusty and breathless Colonel Ponsonby of the 12th Light Dragoons galloped in with urgent despatches for the army commander. Napoleon had abdicated. Europe was at peace. Six hard, long years of campaigning were at an end.

The news spread through the divisional lines and men stopped in their tracks and stared at each other. Some went immediately to the drink shops and wine cellars. Some sat quite still and grinned at each other, thankful that they had survived. Some wrote letters for home and some just walked about the streets and gardens, revelling in their new state - no more hard commons, no more surprise attacks and the fury of death or injury.

A well-tuned, superbly led military machine had come to a full stop with victory over a powerful enemy.

In the next few weeks the cavalry trotted and walked its way across France to Calais and Boulogne, to embark for the home country.

The infantry, some marching across the sunny fields of France, some making a leisurely journey by river barge, assembled at Bordeaux to await the transport ships for England.

Jack felt a sudden poignancy as he watched the sad sight of dozens of Spanish and Portuguese women being parted from their British soldiers by staff officers and provost corps. Official wives were, of course, allowed to return with their husbands; but the hundreds of unofficial liaisons that had developed over the years, many like Jack and Rosa's, with young children in attendance, were irregular and had no place in the army's system.

Tearful women were set loose to find their own way back across hundreds of miles to their homes with nothing more than the clothes they wore and a hurriedly passed purse of coins to keep them from starving.

This might have been Jack's situation had Rosa lived to see the peace. In some ways he felt relieved that a harsh fate had solved this problem for him.

Molly had made Jack's child her own responsibility and it would have taken more than Wellington's entire army to have parted her from the infant. She dressed him in neat clothes of her own making, fed him regularly and lavished more care and attention than had ever been the lot of her own children in her confused and wandering past.

The three friends sorted out their belongings on the quayside when their turn was due for a ship; the baby was in their care – now named Thomas Wheeler to the pride and delight of the little Irishman. Molly had wisely sold all but the most portable of their baggage and the trio had between them nearly £600 in gold coin.

Lying in the sun on the slow river barges and now boarding a man o' war that would have them on Portsmouth hard within a week, the trio endlessly discussed their future. Sergeant Hooper had warned them to have no illusions about the life that would await the returning veterans. Already tales had filtered back from the first to step ashore in England - tales of twenty-four hour rejoicing, ale houses with open doors and a gratified but parsimonious government, anxious to pay off and sign off its soldiers and return them to the gutter.

Like the cold light of a dawn hangover, the Peninsular campaigners realised that they were fighting men in a country now dedicated to the arts of peace.

"On your way, soldier," was the usual cry as wounded and soon penniless redcoats hobbled off to search for work, to beg in the streets or return to their native villages in the hopes of picking up the threads of an old calling or to offer their services in the harvest fields.

Now on the broad deck of a ship of the line, Jack raised the question once again. "I've a craft to go back to and money besides. We could have a home built between us—a fine house with rooms for all. Molly could raise young laddy here and you, Tom, could join me in my work. We might open a shop together. There's all manner of things we might do; maybe set up a carrier's business or buy a field or two for sheep raising."

Molly's eyes gleamed at the thought of a domestic hearth at last - a place to keep her own things and a child to rear and work for. But Tom was realistic. "We've been wanderin' for years, Jacko," he said. "Wanderin' and havin' fun where we took it. I'm not yet forty and I could never settle down to a quiet little village such as yours. They say there's great manufactories startin' in the North of England with high wages and plenty to eat and drink. I'd like to take a look at these first and try my hand in one of them big cities."

They discussed the question on and off through an uneventful voyage until they landed at Portsmouth town. Bands played them up to the barracks into which they had first marched over three years before.

A few speeches from their officers, the drawing of their arrears of pay and the veterans were free to crowd into a sutler's shed to drink their first pots of English ale. Thick tobacco smoke almost obscured the feeble light of the oil lamps, and pots of ale were drawn in an endless stream as old comrades bade farewell to each other.

"An alehouse for me with me winnings from Vitoria—I'm back to the pits, a collier of Derbyshire, that's me—me father's old farm'll be right tame after this little lot—try me luck in London town—back to the master's service, if he'll have me—a mail coach guard if they'll have me, wi' a blunderbuss instead of old Brown Bess!"

Sergeant Hooper came across with two foaming cans for Jack and Tom. "Well, lads. End of the road, eh! What a road we've took together since you first came through that gate and into my squad here. Ay! I've made good soldiers of you, though you've never been a saint in the scarlet coat, have you, Tom Eagan?"

A few laughs, some firm handshakes and the army of the Peninsular went its separate ways.

Jack booked seats and paid in gold for the night mail coach to Dorchester. It was a fine, clear night in June with darkness not until after nine o'clock. The two men perched on the top of the swaying vehicle while Molly slept inside with the child. As they bowled through the New Forest and dawn replaced the moonlight, they talked quietly of nights of danger and discomfort, or rioting and revels that they had known in that harsh land to the south.

With stops for meals and changing of horses, it was mid-morning before they set down at the Royal George in busy Dorchester.

Jack was for buying a handcart for their luggage to set off for his home in Winterbourne, but the usual thirst of Tom led them into a tavern where they fell in with a carrier taking market purchases back to the villages. He'd take them all for a guinea and glad to help any soldiers of the King home from England's wars.

It was a warm evening with several hours of daylight left when Jack and his friends drew up before the Wheeler cottage. He took his son from Molly and slowly looked up and down the village street. Young villagers and their elders came running from both ends. The entire custom of The George turned out to a man and the veterans were soon surrounded by an excited crowd.

Jack turned to his cottage as the door opened and his mother stood there and stared at him. Younger children rushed past her skirts to summon their father from the sheepfolds. The older woman came slowly forward, embraced her bronzed and lean faced son, then quietly took the child from his shoulders and held it tightly to her. She then burst into a flood of tears to the emotional delight of her crowd of neighbours.

That night the village was a blaze of candlelight and a bustle of excitement and activity. A feast was prepared at The George and Jack gave enough money to the landlord to underwrite ale and food for the entire community.

Mrs Wheeler herself prepared a neat and spotless bedroom for the Eagans who were told to stay as long as they wished.

A child's wooden cot was scrubbed and dried, then fitted with clean linen bedclothes for the young Thomas.

At The George the entire village, squire, parson, farmers, shepherds, the carrier (who postponed his other calls for the day) and even the local children were there to eat, drink and cheer the three veterans and their young supernumerary who had returned from Wellington's army.

Over the next few weeks, Jack slowly settled back into the old routine of village life. Another man had been working as part-time cobbler, but he gladly returned to the more robust work of his father's blacksmith's shop and left Jack to pick up his original trade.

Molly and Tom pottered about, spending their money in periodic trips to Dorchester and occasionally livening up the evenings at The George.

All over England the victory was celebrated from the lavish spectacular in London's Hyde Park, arranged by the Prince Regent himself, to village feasting such as at Winterbourne where the squire threw open his barns and had oxen roasted and ale by the barrel. Jack and Tom were guests of honour together with some of the shepherd boys who had enlisted with them and were now full grown men with the light of much experience in their eyes.

Slowly and surely Mrs Wheeler took over the care of little Tom. At first Molly resisted with good humour, but as she and Tom spent more time on trips that took them further afield – sometimes for days on end – so she relinquished her right to the child.

Late one night Jack heard an argument in the Eagans' bedroom - an argument that rose and fell from low murmuring to violent outbursts.

Next morning, while washing at the pump in the yard, Jack was joined by Molly and Tom. They were both dressed in their best clothes and Tom was leading a sprightly young forest pony he had bought from a horse dealer the previous night.

"We're on our way, Jack," said Molly in her forthright manner. "On our way to the north with our baggage an' what's left of our bit o' money."

"Ay, Jacko. We talked it over last night an' made up our minds," said Tom.

"Talked it over?" said Jack. "I thought you was having a fight by the sound of it. But why go?"

Molly came close to him and spoke quietly. "We're travellers, Jack. Wandering vagabonds all our life and likely to stay that way. This little runt o' mine reckons he can make his fortune at them mills in the north an' if he goes then old Molly goes too, if only to see he don't kill himself one dark and drunken night. It's been good stayin' here, Jack, but we don't belong in this quiet life. I thought maybe I'd settle down to a house o' my own an' a few bits an' things. I will one day, but right now his feet are itching for new roads an' he's still my man for all his terrible ways."

Jack took both their hands for a moment. "Come in and I'll get you breakfast before the others are up."

They went in and he and Molly fried bacon and bread while Tom piled stores on a pack saddle for the pony.

Mrs Wheeler appeared and accepted the situation with a polite silence.

The sun was fully up when Tom led the pony out of the yard and the three old friends stood in the centre of the village street. Mrs Wheeler went inside to bring out the sleepy child. She put the boy on her son's shoulders and smiled a farewell at the Irish couple. Then she discreetly went back into the cottage.

"Well Tom," said Jack. "I joined for adventure and I got it. I wouldn't do it again for all the gold in Spain but by God you were a good mate o' mine and I'm proud to have known you."

As they shook hands, Tom grinned broadly. "Ah, Jacko! 'Twas a rare old time or two we had together an' no mistake. I'll see ye again one day if I keeps out o' gaol. Now here's a little something I always meant the little fella to have. 'Twill be right for him when he's full grown an' I got it for free off a dead Frenchy general, so nobody's the loser."

He produced from his pocket a magnificent gold watch with a finely worked chain. Jack took the watch and held it up to the child's ear to listen to the ticking.

Molly gave Jack one of her great bear hugs and the tough Irishwoman had tears on her cheeks.

"God bless you, Jack an' the little lad. I've loved you like me own and I did her too. She were a good woman to you and you're to see that boy brought up right for her sake. Good schoolin' and a steady home for him. Remember us poor wanderin' folk—only you could make Irish Molly weep like a maid."

She turned away and Tom heaved her up on to the already overladen pony. "Come on, ye great Clonmel cow. Get your fat legs over that fine beast an' we're away!"

She swiped at him with a leather bag. "Easy now, you redcoat tosspot. I'm a fine lady on a fine horse, so just you mind your manners!"

Tom took a half-empty bottle from his pocket and took a swig that finished the lot. "Here's to you, Jack an' me little namesake there. Arrah there! Off we go! To Badajoz or hell, I care not which!"

He tossed the bottle over the hedge, gave the pony a slap on the rump and they ambled off up the village street, climbing to the slight hill at the top. At the bend they turned and waved before disappearing into the few remaining shreds of morning mist.

Jack stood with the silent, wide-eyed child on his shoulders for several minutes. Then he lowered his son gently to the ground, took his tiny hand into his own and they walked slowly through the cottage front door.

THE END